The Day Before Tomorrow

Twentieth Century Scottish Women's Fiction
Series Editor: Anne McManus Scriven,
Centre for Scottish Cultural Studies,
University of Strathclyde

Moira Burgess

The Day Before Tomorrow

with an Introduction by
Douglas Gifford

and a new Afterword by the author

Kennedy & Boyd

Kennedy & Boyd
an imprint of
Zeticula
57 St Vincent Crescent
Glasgow
G3 8NQ
Scotland.

http://www.kennedyandboyd.co.uk
admin@kennedyandboyd.co.uk

First published in 1971 By Wm Collins
Copyright © Moira Burgess 1971, 2009
Afterword © Moira Burgess 1971, 2009
Introduction Copyright © Douglas Gifford 2009

ISBN-13 978-1-904999-64 5 Paperback
ISBN-10   1-904999-64-6 Paperback

Introduction

In *The Glasgow Novel*, her groundbreaking bibliography and discussion (three editions (1972-1999), Moira Burgess gave us by far the fullest and richest account of Glasgow's fiction, ranging from Scott's evocative Glasgow scenes in *Rob Roy* (1818) and John Galt's *The Entail* (1822) to Sarah Tytler's *St Mungo's City* (1884) and the great novelists of Glasgow in the twentieth century, from Catherine Carswell, George Blake and Guy McCrone between the wars to the burgeoning period of the second half of the century of Robin Jenkins, Archie Hind, George Friel, William McIlvanney, Alastair Gray, James Kelman and Alison Kennedy, and so many others. Her study became her rich critical study *Imagine a City: Glasgow in Fiction* (1998), in which she showed how contemporary writers like Gray had developed the Glasgow novel into a highly mature form, worthy of international respect.

With typical and unnecessary modesty, she omits her *The Day Before Tomorrow* (1971), her own Glasgow novel, from this later study; and in *The Glasgow Novel*, in her own short entry she self-deprecatingly criticises (again, unnecessarily) the novel's 'slightly intrusive thriller plot'. Another author would have emphasized this novel's substantial contribution to Glasgow fiction – and with hindsight we can now see that the work belongs with that period of recovery in Scottish literature generally, from the mid-'sixties on, with the emergence of the poetry and fiction of major writers like Norman MacCaig, George Mackay Brown and Iain Crichton Smith. The contribution of Glasgow writers to this was prominent, from Edwin Morgan to Robin Jenkins, and George Friel to William McIlvanney, and outstandingly with Archie Hind's *The Dear Green Place* in 1966. With its clear love of the city's atmosphere and 'the speak' of its people– but equally clear recognition of older Glasgow slum horrors – we can see now that *The Day Before Tomorrow* was an important part of the revival, placing itself in the tradition of George Blake's *The Shipbuilders* (1935) and *The Dear Green Place*.

Deceptively unpretentious in its subtle circling around several archetypal Glasgow lives over a week of Saturday to Saturday, with the significant changes in the main characters during a sweltering heatwave, Burgess manages to de-prioritise the central fact that the novel moves around two horrific murders. Thus she cleverly comments on, yet sidesteps, an entire Glasgow genre, that of the *No Mean City* and *Cut and Run* category, in which novelists controversially exploited Glasgow's early twentieth-century image. (McIlvanney was to do something of the sort with his *Laidlaw* novels, (1977, 1983), but with greater allegiance to the detective genre.)

The Day Before Tomorrow is a carefully crafted novel, whose subtleties and persuasive human analyses become fully appreciated in a second reading, where understated touches of authorial direction can be enjoyed more fully. In an earlier review I described it thus:

...a thickly textured version of Glasgow's slum Cowcaddens, using the threat to the community of a serial killer to explore community responses in ways which, while seeing all the bleak features of her subjects, finds redemption in human relations in a finally positive human setting...

I'm grateful for the chance to revise this less than appropriate description of the part of Glasgow Burgess calls 'the Claggans'. Re-reading has made me see just how much more needs to be said – and corrected.

Corrections first – I'm now pretty sure that the Cowcaddens are a few miles off where the novel takes place, if indeed the novel is being specific at all. At times the setting seems to suggest the decaying Gorbals, on the south side of the river, but at others setting suggesting old Partick, with the river and Kelvingrove park not far off and playing a central part in the drama, with the chilling figure of Quinn lounging at the high platform of its flagpole at the heart of the novel. But apart from this, there are no secure guidelines - so it can be argued that, as with Kelman's Glasgow novels, the leaving out of specific place-naming leaves the reader free to imagine their own Glasgow.[1]

Again, re-reading made this reader see the choice of not-so-usually violent working class West end setting as another way of side-stepping Glasgow cliché. Psychopathic Quinn may be the dark sub-text of this novel, but it is really about a linked group, around a main dozen in all, of recognisable Glasgow people – mainly from the slum tenements which are being pulled down during the novel's time, but with deft insights into the lives of other social levels. As a librarian herself, Burgess's picture of long-suffering librarians who have to put up with smelly old men using their library as a place of rest is wickedly convincing – as is her cameo picture of a family in a leafy residential posh area – Hyndland? Bearsden? There are echoes of the perspectives of George Friel and Robin Jenkins in her sly, yet sympathetic satire.

But the heart of the novel is her creation of Mrs Sheehan – ageing, fat, withering through the death of her husband and the leaving of her children, one to marriage and a high-rise flat, the other to London. She sighs in her decaying tenement, a woman of immense human sympathies, but lacking anywhere to give them – till suddenly life hands her back not only her darling, impulsive and lovable Bernadette (Bernie), but Bernie's baby. And not only has she now to care for them, but next door a trio in crisis increasingly turns to her. Old Brady, smelly, drunk, cannot accept the death of his wife Rose; left to fend for themselves are Kieron and his younger brother, the innocent, Danny. These are challenges, but Mrs Sheehan thrives upon them, since they give her life meaning.

Thus the novel has two counter-currents. The one which matters is Mrs Sheehan's, a lovely story of humanity and redemption; the other, about which Burgess cleverly leaves false scents and red herrings, is a slow moving tide of evil, as The Claggans begins to realise that a serial killer is in its midst. The reader first suspects Eugene Carty, a pale, sex-haunted adolescent with a horrid old mother; or old Brady, who horrifies strange girls by hallucinating that are they are his dead Rose, watched suspiciously by local gossips as he shambles by. But Burgess's slow development of the golden-haired, utterly emotionless Quinn takes us from seeing him in the library in contrast to its dossers to the point where we realise that he is pure evil, devoid of humanity, so that Carty and Brady lapse into their roles as simple human tragedies and misfits. It is the strength of this novel, however, that its whodunit aspect is itself something of a red herring, since Burgess's aim is to show that the countless stories of mundane humanity triumph over random horror. For Mrs Sheehan's is not the only example of redemption; it is also Bernie's as her child finds a family, and Kieron's, as he finds Bernie, and vulnerable innocent Danny, as he finds protectors – and even old Brady's, as somehow his scattered alcoholic wits become the means of Quinn's downfall.

There is however no manipulation to rosy conclusions for others; Eugene Carty emerges as a lost and hyper-sensitive soul who deserves sympathy rather than condemnation; he certainly doesn't deserve either his mother or his ghastly end. Particularly moving, moreover, is the story of middle-class Helen, bright and full of energy to give to the world, privileged, yet convincingly portrayed as a hugely gifted idealist, who wants to take music and colour down to The Claggans. Yes, she condescends, and yes, her naivete almost angers – but Burgess suggests that she has indeed so much to offer and live for. Re-reading made me feel just how appallingly random and tragic Helen's story is – not just for herself, but for her mother, who didn't really bother to know exactly where her daughter was going that fateful night, and for her father, who will have to live forever with the thought that if he'd not preferred golf to driving his darling daughter…

So the novel's week is a week of watersheds. Mrs Sheehan loses her dream of going back to the countryside, where she grew up; Bernie loses her freedom, tied as she is to her baby; the young librarian Lisa loses any last innocence and dreams as she realises how wrong she was to idealise Quinn – will she ever trust men entirely again? And of course Eugene and Helen – and their families – lose everything. It's hard for Burgess then to convince us that Claggans will recover, but somehow she does. And this is where the novel's title begins to resonate. At the basic level, 'the day before tomorrow' is a working-man's phrase for the day before payday, and thus the lean time before relief and escape. Mrs Sheehan plays with the phrase in the novel, but for us it resonates differently, as indeed each of the seven days here is a day before tomorrow, darkening and lightening according to perspective. In another sense it's an implied question about what tomorrow will bring, and the day-to-day accounts emphasize this randomness. But finally, it's about how, despite this randomness, Mrs Sheehan's encompassing human love can win through to the point where, giving love, she is given love back. The close leaves her with poor Danny's head resting on her knee, dependant; yet he gives her release, since, as her cottage-dream has died, he reconciles her to leaving the sordid Claggans for a clean high-rise flat, like that of her other daughter Annie. Mrs Sheehan has a phobia regarding their lifts; Danny however thinks them rare fun; and Mrs Sheehan's and the novel's closing words, 'well now…you'll need to teach me tomorrow' optimistically round out the motif of 'tomorrow' so subtly maintained throughout.

The novel's structure deserves comment. Each day is divided into sections – but not in any clockwork fashion (for example, Tuesday is one single section, where Wednesday has six). This reflects the theme of randomness, but also avoids any sense of artificiality, enabling Burgess to almost casually develop her circles of acquaintance. She sometimes uses the image of a chessboard in her authorial overview of the city's innumerable and random games of life, but a chessboard in which the real moves are being made by unknowable forces. But the overall effect is strong and clear. By giving us seven days before tomorrow, and helping us to see them if not simultaneously, at least holistically, there is a pervasive sense that what is apparently random may in fact be a drama with meaning, however indecipherable that meaning may be to the actors within it. In the end I had the sense almost of a play working itself out through discrete scenes and acts – a play which reminded me of another fine writer, this time for the stage – Ena Lamont Stewart, whose powerful drama of Glasgow slum life, *Men Should Weep* (1947), presented just such an interweaving of ordinary, yet so important, lives. Most striking of all, however – and perhaps to be expected from the historian of urban Scottish fiction – is Burgess's rich awareness of her Glasgow, and the imagined Glasgow of her forerunners and contemporaries. Her novel is an enduring part of that heritage.

Douglas Gifford
April 2009

Saturday

1

After killing young Frances Callaghan the murderer went home to bed, moving quickly, along with the darting rats, between middens and washhouses and among the broken teeth of derelict tenements, through the summer night warm and soft as milk. In his airless room, with the window closed against the seeping demolition dust, he slept heavily as after the act of love. He woke late with a headache and a dirty mouth, but by early afternoon he had made up time, and went into his local public library like many another person with nothing special to do. Mrs Sheehan, going to visit her married daughter, passed him in the street, though of course she didn't know who he was.

She walked past without even seeing him. She found herself standing at the bus-stop down by the Gogo Café without any clear memory of having got there. That had happened more than once recently, and she thought, Maybe I'm going daft at last. Though, thinking that, she felt a bit more like herself.

But there was a change in her, no doubt about it. She stood at the bus-stop, a fat breathless old woman in a flowery print dress: into her head came the memory of a day nearly two years ago, before her youngest daughter Bernie went away. They had been standing, the two of them, at another bus-stop on the way back from the shops, arms full of packages, giggling over something silly, when a woman coming the other way had jostled them nearly into the gutter and gone on without saying sorry.

Mrs Sheehan had frowned as she looked after the woman: 'God love her, Bernie, she's not well. Did you not see the colour of her face?'

Young Bernie had laughed. 'Oh Mammy! See if a mad razor-slasher came down the street? You'd say poor soul, the terrible bellyache he must have.'

But these last few months people for Mrs Sheehan were just

people in the lump. She did her bit of shopping with them, and washed floors for them, and walked past without seeing them in the crumbling streets of the Claggans. A muddled greyness hung round the rim of her sight, like the grey mist you moved in when you were very tired or very unhappy. She wasn't any more tired than usual, and she had no special reason for being unhappy. Peter was dead a year now, and it was even longer since Bernie went away to the nursing in London. Plenty of time to get used to being alone. Only it was funny how it hung on, the habit of turning, in her quiet empty house, to say 'Wait till you hear who I saw today!'

And the heat-wave didn't help. From the dank smelly chill of the close you stepped straight into the baking street, so that your eyes winced shut and your dry throat nipped with the dust. Up the street and down the street marched the tenements, blind windows and scabby grey walls. You never noticed them much in winter, when everything was grey anyway and your head was down against the sleety wind. But when the hot sky was blue and the heat pulsed back from the pavements, then you felt the tall houses closing you in.

'Why the hell,' said Mrs Sheehan, 'anybody lives in this place at all.'

But her bus came along, and, heaving herself aboard, searching for her fare, settling into the sticky seat as she was bumped over the hard hot streets, she lost that thought: though it was one that had come to her strangely often at odd times in the last few weeks.

The city was changed by summer. The hot silver sky coaxed its grey heart open like a rose, and out into the parks came young mothers in short frocks with bare babies jumping in their prams. Men squatted at the close-mouths, women leaned on cushions at their windows two floors up, little girls set up shop and hospital games along the slaty pavements, all as if there was no other weather than this and no other way to live.

By lunch-time the policemen had their jackets off. That changed the city amazingly, the tough young men in their suddenly rakish caps and clean blue shirts with the sleeves precisely folded. They were like musical-comedy policemen: the dark nights of knives and screams and running footsteps in the back-courts were long ago and in another town.

In this fresh gay summer city Frances Callaghan's body was discovered by a gang of little girls, fortunately so young that they ran and told their mammies there was a wumman sleeping in the washhouse. Mrs Sheehan, jolting hotly on the bus, saw at the end of the street the grim little crowd, the police-cars and the ambulance. Trouble for someone: time was when that would have moved her to a quick prayer as her stomach twisted in sympathy with the unknown. But the bus jerked on and she stared unseeing out at the grey streets reeling by. The grey cobwebs clung round her, smothering prayers and feelings and all.

2

The news broke too late for the noon papers. Until four o'clock the old men in the reading-room dozed on, waking occasionally to wipe eyes and noses on greyish rags and trace with horny bent fingers the small print of the race-cards. The sun struck in through the high narrow windows above the reading-slopes, stirring up a golden dust in the air.

Brady shambled up the street, hot in his long filthy grey coat. You would think a man with a son at work could get a coat that wouldn't chitter his guts out in winter and fry the hide off him in summer. At every step the bottle in his pocket jolted against his dragging leg: it was no comfort, being empty. Too early to go for a refill. Too soon even to go home for tea. You would think a man could go home on a Saturday and expect something on the table, not when Lord Muck came home from the baths. Across his path fell the blocky shadow of the public library, not particularly inviting on a hot summer day, but a place to sit till opening time. Brady cleared his throat, spat on the steps and limped in.

The big reading-room with the sun streaming in was a box of dusty gold. Brady screwed up his weak eyes, and in a frame of opaque gold he saw the calm oval face and high-piled blonde hair of his young wife Rose. He cried out and crossed himself, but the sign was a fumble of a fuddled rheumatic hand, and the cry was only the phlegmy croak you expect from dirty old men.

The young face turned towards him and the blue eyes opened

wide. Of course it was not Rose, because Rose was three months dead. It was the new library lassie. She was pretty and blonde, but like most new ones she had a snippy look about her. Brady picked up a magazine at random and hunched into the nearest chair.

He did not read. He sank his head between his shoulders and squinted up at the bonnie fair girl. Rose thirty years ago, as fair and calm as this lassie, waved him off to the war. When he came back, what with bombs and rationing and the factory, a dredging of grey had already spoiled her shining hair and the first lines had set hard between her eyebrows. This lassie was no more than nineteen, and she had no lines yet, but she would get them if she frowned like that. She had felt him staring at her, and she didn't like it. Brady humped his shoulder over the yellow-paged magazine and tracked his finger along unmeaning words.

The swing-door chunked. A gust of spices and grease, a slap on the hard chair next to Brady: old Moses sat down, a green sports edition rolled in his dirty fist.

'Did ye see this, Pat?'

The girl behind the counter frowned more severely. Brady jerked his head towards her and twisted his face at Moses.

'Ah, God help her,' said Moses. 'If that's a' she has tae worry about.' He flattened out his paper on the desk and slanted up at Brady his beautiful dark eyes under their heavy grizzled brows. 'It's another murder,' he said.

Brady rubbed his red eyelids and focused on the thick Saturday headlines. ANOTHER CLAGGANS SEX HORROR, they said. LINK WITH ALICE KILLING? Moses drew a black-rimmed finger under the important bits. The naked body of Frances Callaghan (18), pretty waitress at the popular Gogo Cafe in the city's Claggans district, was found this morning in a disused washhouse . . .'

'It's the same as yon other lassie,' breathed Moses in his ear. His strong old face was wrinkled up in distress. 'The Alice yin, the barmaid that was raped doon at the Regent Dock. They hivny got the dirty bastard yet.'

A restlessness was spreading among the old men. Mad Mac with his cap on backwards had come in at a shuffling run, clutching the rival pink Saturday paper. He bent over Granda, who woke with a spraying snort. The news travelled from table to table, from trembling old mouth to gleaming old eye. There was murmuring, there was rumour: the frowning girl turned her head to and fro like a nervous filly. Saturday afternoon wasn't the time for serious readers, or the snippity housewives who tutted and shushed; but there was a young salesman across the room at a corner table whose annoyance was beginning to show. He looked up from his order books and cleared his throat and tapped his pencil end over end on the table, his mouth drawn straight and tight. He was a stickler for the rule-book, you could see that, not one to be soothed with an apologetic smile, though the flustered girl as a last resort was trying that too. But something had come into the reading-room that outranked the silence rule.

Brady read slowly, 'The killer who likes young blonde girls . . .' He said, 'I'm gonny show this to that lassie. She'll need tae watch.'

'Ach, Pat, ye're aff yer nut.' But Brady had picked up the paper, and Moses, grumbling, heaved himself to his feet. It was his paper, after all. Together they carried it to the counter and spread it in front of the girl, who reluctantly bent her head to read.

'Second in three weeks,' Moses pointed out.

'Lassies isny safe thae days,' said Brady. Close up she was not so much like Rose, of course. He said, 'You'll need tae watch, miss. It says he likes blondes.'

She looked up sharply at that and he saw he had gone too far; but the librarian, Miss Grierson, came through the door from the lending department and said, 'I'll finish up here, Lisa. Can you help them at the front counter?'

'Another lassie raped, missis,' croaked old Moses, a little above himself. Miss Grierson raised her eyebrows and said, 'Yes, well, gentlemen, only fifteen minutes left to select your weekend reading.' Old Moses, who didn't have library tickets, huffily folded up his newspaper and went over to wake Jamie Ratface, who had slept through it all.

'Naebody's gonny rape her, anyway,' he observed, 'unless they get paid for it,' but he did not mean it enough to say it aloud.

Brady watched the blonde girl walk through to the lending library. She was a tall girl, well-made, with a good body: Rose had been too narrow there. All the trouble carrying and losing weans, ending up with only Kieron and Danny seven years apart. After Danny he knew that would have to be the lot. Going away had seemed like the best thing then: looking for work, that was the idea. He never meant to go on the road. Nobody ever meant to.

And somewhere in those hard years the start of the thing that killed her. He on his road, and she on hers; and that bone-cold evening in Lent when he came home and stared aghast at the husk of a woman in the kitchen bed.

He thought he would get a cowboy for the week-end. He had lost his tickets of course, but the lassies wereny bad about it sometimes. Only that blonde bitch, she had a snippy look.

3

The lights were off in the children's section and the staff workroom; that side of the library was shadowed by high broken buildings, a premature blue twilight creeping in from the ceiling corners. Lisa, waiting for the last stragglers to choose their books, turned over an abandoned newspaper on the counter.

It was a later edition than Moses'. There was a blurry photograph of Frances Callaghan beside one of the barmaid Alice Tribe, and CLAGGANS MURDERS - MANIAC ? was the headline. The girls had been eighteen and nineteen: even in the blotched blown-up snaps you could see some resemblance between them, oval faces and long pale hair. Both had been walking home alone late at night, though in June it would hardly have been dark. The sub-editor had repeated his favourite maxim about the killer liking young blondes.

Lisa read on. They had been attacked in lonely streets. They had been savagely beaten about the head. They had been raped. There was something about the tone of the report that hinted at worse horrors still. She frowned forbiddingly as she read, and felt a deep small fluttering, partly guilty, not wholly unknown, but unexpected at this moment. She still read on.

'Excuse me, miss,' said Eugene Carty humbly.

He had laid his tickets on the counter, so that his name and face registered together with Lisa. A face you might notice, anyway, strangely pale between the flat black rim of smoothed-down hair and the square line of the jaw. You might notice the address too, in the heart of the old Claggans slums; and you could hardly help noticing that, when he asked for the book he wanted, he did so in a hoarse whisper, bright-eyed.

It didn't worry Lisa now: she placed him in a category, that was all. When he added softly 'And while you're in there, miss—' she placed him in it a little more firmly. Miss Grierson had been known to remark chattily, 'You know, if they were really pornography we wouldn't have them,' but Miss Grierson could get away with it. Lisa went into the reserve stock room, found the books he wanted and brought them back to the counter. He said earnestly, 'Thank you very much, miss,' but she looked away from his eager eyes and his warm wet mouth.

The next reader was the young salesman from the reading-room, blond and polite, his order books tucked under one arm and his week-end war, crime and travel under the other. The name on his tickets was Quinn, just Quinn. Probably his writing was so bad that the junior had given up at that. Yet there was nothing untidy about the rest of him; in the shuffle of last-minute borrowers he was unusually smart, grey suit, thick gold cap of hair well-brushed, broad clean hands well-kept. Lisa, opening and stamping his books with the automatism of Saturday counter duty, looked up at him under her thick eyelashes and smiled shyly. He was a Saturday regular, but she still felt a little in awe of him, handsome and calm and cold. He had been irritated by all that noise in the reading-room, and no wonder; but he showed no trace of annoyance now, nor of any particular emotion at all. At least he hadn't complained to Miss Grierson. Into her smile she tried to put, as well as apology, thanks for that.

She might as well, she thought, not have bothered. He didn't smile back: of course, as she ought to have remembered, he never did. But he looked very straight at her, and she dropped her eyes before his clear light-blue stare.

'I've lost ma tickets,' announced the last reader. To make matters worse, it was one of the filthy old men from the reading-room, huddled in a grey coat that was ready to walk off without him.

Lisa sighed. 'Are you sure?'

'Sure I'm sure.'

The smell at close quarters was overpowering: when he spoke, rivulets of saliva slipped down his bristly chin. Lisa, after a day's work, hardly felt up to an argument. 'All right,' she said. 'We'll give you duplicates. What's your name?'

'Patrick Brady.'

As she scribbled it on a card and opened his two books he complained, 'There's never nae bloody cowboys in this liberry.'

'That's two you've got there.'

'There's never none I hivny read,' persisted Brady. 'I've read thur, see?'

Indeed there was a deeply-pencilled B on each title-page. 'You're not supposed,' said Lisa, 'to write in the books.'

'How else would I ken I'd read them?' said Brady.

'Well, it's closing time,' said Lisa, 'so you'll just have to read them again, and she had the books stamped before he could object. 'Some of them,' she said to Miss Grierson, coming through from die reading-room, 'you'd think they hadn't homes to go to.' The door had not quite closed behind Brady.

'Maybe they haven't,' said Miss Grierson unexpectedly. Lisa looked at her to see if she was joking. Brady, standing on the steps stuffing a western into either pocket of his calf-length grey coat, was so perfectly the old man on the park bench, greasy hair, muffler, broken boots and all.

'Oh, I dare say they have really.' Miss Grierson flicked up the light-switches. 'Are you coming for the number seven, Lisa?'

'No, I'll walk across the park,' Lisa said.

'Is that all right?' Miss Grierson, unusually, was a little hesitant. 'You don't think you should take the bus round? I mean, you know—'

'Oh, the maniac?' said Lisa. 'It's still six hours to sunset. Don't you think I'll make it?'

She stood outside the library to pull on her white gloves, a big young blonde girl in a summer-short pink cotton dress. Brady, the last customer, had not got very far. He threw her a glance over his shoulder and limped off along the side of the library with his dislocated walk. Eugene Carty came out of the public lavatory so handily placed next door and walked quickly away, after Brady, down to the docks and the slums which Lisa skirted each morning by bus, her ticket held in her gloved hand.

The warm tired air of a city Saturday afternoon frayed the fair hair across her cheek as she turned away from them into the park. She pushed the hair back pettishly. The hot weather had got them all going at work; everyone had been on edge, impatient with the sweaty people who had to have their romances and westerns come rain or shine. The other junior had at least been buoyed up by the prospect of her Saturday date, but Lisa was between boy-friends. What had she to look forward to tonight? Salad for tea, and a walk round the buildings with her father and mother.

Through the park railings she caught a flicker of grey, the glint of a gold head: the quiet young salesman with the light-blue eyes, calmly walking home. He was going down into the Glaggans too, although he didn't look a Claggans type. Perhaps he was in digs there. Probably he hated it, down there among the drunks and the razors and the broken bottles which (everybody knew) made up Saturday night in the Claggans. 'How do you like your digs?' she could say to him, some day, perhaps

Silly Lisa, you know you'll do no such thing. Still, he was something to think about, mmm yes he was, in the warm sleepy evening when it was a shame to be walking alone. At least he was a nice clean normal polite young man, and after a Saturday in the Claggans reading-room you were glad to think about somebody like that for a change. Lisa thought about him, vague pleasing thoughts, while the park slipped past her in a rosy haze. Lost in the green smell of cut grass and the tamed fire of the rhododendrons was that silly remark of Miss Grierson's, which had brushed across her mind again there on the library steps ... Maybe they haven't ...

But Eugene Carty had a home to go to. In the lavatory he had unfolded from his inside pocket the paper covers of two eminently respectable books, one on engineering and one on the French Revolution, and shrouded in them the two books from the library's reserve stock room. He had no spare jacket for his third book, which he had picked up earlier that afternoon in a city bookshop. He knew he would want to read it first: it offered more immediate excitement than you could expect from the library. After some thought he stripped off its lurid jacket and tore it up, devoting special care to certain areas which he shredded into scraps smaller than his broad thumbnail. He scattered the shreds in the corner of the lavatory, for want of a litterbin, and the book, now demure in its drab cloth cover, went into his pocket.

Then he went home; and his mother greeted him with the frying-pan in her hand and told him to eat up quickly and put on a clean collar and help her down to confession. She hoped, she added, that he would never know what it was to be dependent on your children for the least wee thing, aye, for the very chance to go and confess your sins to holy God. Eugene, who knew better than to reply, ate his sausage and egg quickly. He wondered why he bothered going through the pantomime of the book jackets. One book, to his mother, was the same as the next, unless it might be two editions of the missal.

And Quinn had a home to go to. He climbed the three flights of stairs to the single room, which he liked because of its view; he could see, if he had known it, Eugene Carty's bedroom window with its prim net screens, and Brady's close, into which a young dark-haired girl was just then turning, carrying a canvas bag and a heavy, rosy baby.

More to the point, he had a wide view over the Claggans, both the distant skyscrapers on the hill and the old Claggans that was coming down so quickly, rat's nest by rat's nest. Quinn's house, and Carty's and Brady's, stood in the central knot of the Claggans, the last festering place still to be lanced; so his view included broken tenements where children dangerously played, and rubbly waste ground, and half-blocked streets, all down to the thronged and separate world of the docks where masts stood unlikely as trees. He put his black order books on the table, and his three library books on the dresser, and under a cold tap washed his hands free of the sweaty dust of the day. He stood for some time at the window as the city summer evening drew on, and girls in brief flowery dresses took short cuts across the blossoming waste ground.

And Brady had a home to go to, but he did not go there at once. He meant to, vaguely, as much as he meant to do anything; he hobbled down the straight dusty street, his long coat flapping against his lame leg. God, you would think a library the size of Claggans would have better to offer a man than two bloody cowboys he'd read before. Tears of self-pity pricked his sore eyes. And she was a bitch, that blonde one. But pretty. And young. And hellish like Rose.

He signed his forehead automatically as he passed a church: it was Our Lady of Good Aid, so he knew where he was. He was heading for the docks, making straight for the Gogo Cafe.

The Gogo was closed, not so much out of respect for the dead girl as because Mrs Antonio had objected to accommodating a stream of bloody ghouls who weren't even buying a wafer. The police had been there and gone, but the ghouls remained, mostly women, mostly middle-aged, in headscarves and summer coats or cardigans over print dresses and aprons. There were plenty of children, but these had gathered only because they saw a crowd, and were now chasing among the women, climbing walls and lamp-posts, and pushing to its utmost limit the permitted time before they would be skelped, sworn at and sent home. If they had ever known the reason for the gathering, they had forgotten it long ago.

The women might have been in danger of forgetting— so long had passed without event—if they had not taken care to keep the cause alive. They all knew young Francie Callaghan, so that many hours had been spent recalling her childhood and girlhood, her wee innocent face on her First Communion day, and her later dealings with the boys; though she was a nice lassie and not one of your tough wee hairies. They had gone over and over the details of the murder, scanty as these were: the late shift, the goodbye wave at the cafe door, and then no more (for her mother had thought she was staying at her granny's) till the terrible finding. They did not forget to whisper that she had been found with her head all bashed in.

Now the chorus was quiet, watchful for any sign of life or death around the shuttered doors of the Gogo, only occasionally breaking out into another communal cry that it was a bloody sin and they were none of them safe in their beds. They seemed to know, though, that it was not time to go home yet; and as if to reward their vigil, Brady came.

He stopped in alarm; but it would look worse, he realized if he turned and went away. He moved slowly, dragging the leg dislocated years before, along the fringe of the crowd, who turned to watch him closely. He saw none of the Gogo's usual patrons. Most of them he also knew from the reading-room; from the library to the Gogo to the Regent Bar was the daily itinerary of most of the Claggans old men. But the others, Brady realized, had had the sense to stay away. Round the Gogo's door the crowd was thickest, slowing him almost to a standstill. At once a ghoul pounced.

'Wis you coming here, mister?'

'Naw,' said Brady. 'Shut, innit?'

'Dae ye come here often?' enquired a sharp-faced woman, and her fat friend was on the same tack: 'Did ye used tae come here, mister?'

'Naw,' said Brady, his eyes sliding from one to the other. 'Aye. Oh aye. No' recently, though.'

They gathered round him, staring, murmuring, getting ready to identify him. He hunched up one shoulder and turned to scuttle away. The women had closed in behind him.

'When was ye last here, mister?'

'Did ye come a lot?'

'Why did ye stop?'

Brady put down his head and butted through the swelling overalls, the peering headscarves. 'It wasny me,' he said. 'I never seen the lassie.' He knew very well it was the worst thing he could have said.

He was through the crowd at last. He rounded the corner with his awkward hop and headed back the way he had come, past Our Lady's primary school, away from the pointing fingers of the masts and gantries. Oh bloody clever, he told himself. Open your mouth and put your big foot in it. Couldny have done better if ye had done the lassie in. Now some clever dick says he seen Brady in the Gogo yesterday, and where are ye, Patrick?

Brady went home, but not immediately, since it was now past opening time.

5

'You'll love it, though, Mammy,' said Annie, smiling, nodding, glancing round her wee palace; but Mrs Sheehan said, 'No, I'll no'.'

Annie shook her head, bewildered. 'But ye're bound to!' She had such a lovely flat, a prince of a flat that she'd never have got in fifty years down in the old Claggans. This high flat, it appeared, was even a match for Mary Flora's apartment in Toronto; which was a blessing, Mrs Sheehan thought, because when Annie talked about her sister's handsome Canadian husband and swell Canadian house, there had always been a touch of green in her eye. But here were Annie and James very comfortable on the nineteenth floor of a tower block, hot water, central heating, stainless steel sink and all. Mrs Sheehan sat facing the window. You could see neither starlings nor children out of it, not even chimneys, but a deep dizziness of empty air.

'You're bound to like it better than yon! Some nights I canny sleep,' said Annie, 'thinking of you in that rat-heap. The walls running water, aye, they were, last time I was up.' She looked really worried. Mary Flora had been the pretty one, and Bernie the gay one, but Annie was a good-hearted girl.

'And that chimney-head's not safe,' said James, who could be trusted to notice such things.

'And yon cludgie on the stair-' said Annie, wrinkling up her face. 'It's no' healthy, Mammy. It's time the whole place came down.'

Mrs Sheehan said defensively, 'It's no worse than it was when you were all wee at home.'

To her surprise it was the quiet James who said, Oh aye, it's got a lot worse, Ma.'

'The hurricane didny help,' said Mrs Sheehan.

'It's no' even that,' James said. 'The whole place, it's —it's dead, Ma.' He hesitated and said, seeming to swerve to another subject, 'I mind you would aye have flowers in the room when I came up for Annie.'

'They wereny bought special for you,' said Annie smartly. 'Mammy aye had the room nice. Cushion covers, mind? Red curtains.'

'Apples and oranges in a dish,' said James with a gleam in his eye.

They smiled at each other across Mrs Sheehan, refurnishing the cosy courting parlour, seven years old. Mrs Sheehan looked down at her linked hands, seeing what they could not, the room thick under dust and the red curtains looping in rags from their pole.

'But it's hard for you,' said gentle James, 'you being on your own now.'

'Ach, I'm used to that,' said Mrs Sheehan flatly.

'It was different, see,' said Annie eagerly, 'when you had a' your chinas in the other houses. You'd have great company then. But who's left?'

'The Lynches is the new family downstairs,' said Mrs Sheehan. "They'll be hoping to get a new house out o' it. But I haveny even seen her much. She has her hands full wi' the weans.'

'And the Bradys across the landing,' said Annie, 'they're surely there yet?'

'Aye,' said Mrs Sheehan. She tried to think about the Bradys. 'You know Pat came home three months ago, an' then poor Rose died.'

'God be good to her,' said Annie, 'but she lay so long, poor soul.'

'How are they managing,' said James, 'the old man and the two boys on their own?'

Mrs Sheehan wrinkled her brow as if it was a very difficult question. So it was. Oh, she'd waked poor Rose, seen her buried, done the things a neighbour would do; but she had done it all from inside her grey cloud. Now she could hardly remember, in the last few weeks, even seeing the boys Kieron and Danny or the old man Pat Brady. She said to James's question, 'A' right, I think. I couldny really say,' and dimly saw James glance sideways at her as if she had said something strange.

'Time I was getting the tea,' said Annie rather hastily. 'Sit up now off the floor, Pauline.' Six-year-old Pauline stayed sprawled on the floor reading her comic; James rocked back on his chair-legs as Annie went out, and smiled hesitantly at his mother-in-law.

'You'll see the Claggans coming down all round you, Ma,' he said.

'Aye, but they've stopped,' Mrs Sheehan said eagerly. 'They haveny come a yard nearer those last three weeks. Could they have run out o' money, do ye think?'

'Oh aye, that's possible,' said James. He examined the stem of his pipe. 'But they'll start again. Ma, you'll like the high flats once you're in them.'

'No, I'll no', James.'

'Why not?'

'It's —' She could hardly explain it: the teetering height turning her insides to water, the empty windows, the miles of barren corridors and closed doors: and the lift, but that foolish fear she could not really tell even James. 'Och, James, I canny shift. I canny.' She eased her fat bulk in the uncomfortable modern chair. 'Och, but God, what's the use? I'm an old dune wumman. I'll need to do what they say.'

'That's not like you, Ma,' said James.

His quiet voice was warm. It was the first thing for a long time to touch her, deep in the fog that had come down when Peter died. She said in surprise, 'No, it's no', James. Time was I'da said hell mend 'em and got round it someway. But we're a' to be cleared to the high flats, an' that's that.' She glanced at him as he rocked and smoked. 'It's great for Annie, wi' the new kitchen an' bathroom an' a'. But how dae you like it yourself, James?'

'Pauline,' said James, 'run through and see does your mammy need any help.'

As the door closed behind the small girl Mrs Sheehan said, 'Say nae mair, James. It wouldny be right.'

'Och well,' said James. 'Only I could do with a garden, maybe. It doesny bother Annie.'

'You're young,' said Mrs Sheehan. 'You'll move yet.'

'More than likely,' said James with a grin. 'You'll see us in a but an' ben yet. One o' those country cottages, buy it an' do it up with your spare five hundred, you know?'

'Could ye do that, James?' said Mrs Sheehan slowly.

'Oh aye. You get an improvement grant—Hold on, Pauline, that's too heavy for you.'

Rescuing Pauline and helping Annie bring in the rest of the tea-things took up his attention for the next five minutes; and then it was time to sit in, and Mrs Sheehan had never had the chance to ask him any questions. Like 'Did you say five hundred pounds, James?' And of course he couldn't know what an odd excitement he had started in her, talking about a country cottage. How should he? It was a surprise even to herself.

'Sit in, then, Mammy,' said Annie, and Mrs Sheehan made an effort to rise from the deep leather chair. Eventually, with Annie pulling and James pushing and wee Pauline giggling, she was raised like a stranded tanker and docked at the tea-table.

'I'm sorry, hen,' she said. 'It's just the arthritis. It stiffens me up whiles.'

'Aye,' said Annie worriedly. She served out salad and crisps, and poured tea, and then in the middle of passing the bread she said suddenly, 'Have you heard from Bernadette lately?'

'Oh aye,' said Mrs Sheehan immediately. 'Funny ye should ask. Bernie's fine. She's got a great new job in—in one o' the big hospitals down there.'

'Bart's?' said James, interested. 'Or Guy's?'

'Aye, one o' the two o' them,' said Mrs Sheehan. Annie was not satisfied yet, she could see. 'She has to work like a wee Trojan, though. Day duty an' night duty-'

'I thought,' said Annie, 'they got so many days off at the end of their spell on nights. It's a wonder she's never had that and come up to see you.'

'Oh, she's had that of course,' said Mrs Sheehan. 'But och, to come a' this way, it was hardly long enough. An' she got invited home with a friend.' She wondered briefly if she might be overdoing it. 'This lassie, her folk have a big house in Devon an' Cornwall.'

Annie shook her head. 'But has she not had any holidays yet? She's been nursing for eighteen months.'

'She was up a year ago.'

For my da's funeral,' said Annie. 'She could hardly do less. She must be due right holidays this year.'

'Oh aye, she'll be due that,' said Mrs Sheehan. 'I'll likely hear from her any time now.' And she said, 'It's a great view you get up here, Annie. Tell me though, does it never make you dizzy at all?'

In the hallway, after tea, she said for the third time, 'You needny come down with me, Annie.' Even here, with neither windows nor doors to open on to that stomach-griping emptiness, she could feel the height. It tilted her fractionally off the straight; it set a numbness in her head. 'Unless,' she said in desperate hope, 'wee Pauline wants to come down for the ride.'

'Ach, she's watching her programme,' said Annie, looking back over her shoulder at the hunched child on the pouffe. 'You canny stop them, can you? Ach well, James disny like her to go out after tea. You canny see them from up here, and ach, you can understand what he means.'

'Aye,' said Mrs Sheehan. James, decent soul, was drying the dishes; nobody was going to ride down with her in the lift. Her own fault for not asking them. 'Well, nice seeing you, Annie. God bless.'

'Thanks for coming, Mammy.' The lif slid wickedly up to the nineteenth floor and opened its mouth; Mrs Sheehan hurried in, alone. There was time to think of hooligans coming aboard, of small boys tampering with the buttons, of shooting up and down between heaven and earth. To quell her panic she fumbled in her shopper for purse, keys, gloves, and found the jar of lemon curd. She had brought it specially because Annie used to like it; no chance, none, to go back; even if she had dared to operate the buttons again, the gulf of the lift-shaft lengthening above her was final as death. She was a silly old woman, getting into a state like that, and what for? Everybody, everybody was living in high flats nowadays. But she stood and shivered uncontrollably as the lift plunged down.

At the bus-stop she tilted her head back: no sign, on the ranked balconies, of Annie or James or wee Pauline. But you couldn't have seen them anyway from here. Maybe they were waving, maybe Annie was wondering: "She aye brings something home-made, James. I wonder why she never . . . ?' But maybe not; because last time Annie had said an absent thank-you and put the jar aside, and they had had Woolworth's strawberry jam for tea.

6

In the bus her sense returned, and her calmness; she was usually calm. She had time to think of her last muttered conversation with James as she helped to clear the table.

'Did ye say five hundred pounds, James?'

'What was that, Ma?'

'For a country cottage. Five hundred, did ye say?'

'That's what I said.' James was looking at her a bit thoughtfully. 'But mind you, I was only—'

Annie came in then, and Mrs Sheehan said quickly, 'Thanks, James.' There wasn't time to explain what she was thinking about: it was so vague, anyway, that she could hardly have explained it to herself. And men sometimes didn't understand. He might laugh, even James; he might say 'But, Ma, you haven't got five hundred pounds.' Which she hadn't; and she had arthritis, and she lived by scrubbing other folk's floors, and all her days—no, not quite all her days—she had been a fat dusty city sparrow. Supposing somebody dropped five hundred pounds in her lap, what would she do with herself in a country cottage?

But she sat in the bus, more comfortable now as cool evening drew on, and the strangest thoughts ran through her mind. This bus journey was not just an ordinary one. There was a bonus to it that she had discovered on her first visit to Annie's new house. On the point of diving back into the Claggans, the bus pulled up at a stop right on the edge of the escarpment where the high flats gauntly soared: and there, straight ahead, were the hills, the real hills in the north.

That first day, in January, they were delicately white with snow, the sky an angry winter red. They stopped Mrs Sheehan in her tracks. She must have looked funny, a fat old woman sitting straight up in her seat with her mouth open; in fact, the conductress said curiously, 'You all right, hen?' Mrs Sheehan said in a hurry, 'Aye. Oh aye. Just I remembered something.' And that was true; only what she remembered was a long way back, and not, as the conductress would think, that she had forgotten the fish suppers.

Because she had been a country child. She had learned to walk stotting about among the legs of the big soft cows while her father mucked and milked. On the hill behind the farm cottage, in the long sweet summer days, her bare feet had browned and toughened as they sank into bog-myrtle or skipped over tickly sheep-cropped turf. For nearly fifty years she had worn shoes and walked on Claggans plainstones, but she could feel today, in the tender arch between toe and heel, the quiver of short damp grass. And all the time the real hills had been lying in wait for her, to catch her unawares one January day on a Corporation bus; though the funny thing was that she never once remembered noticing them when she was a runabout country child.

Today the hills were a soft blue like the good jersey she had once got for Bernie at a jumble sale, which she had always been sure had been handed in by mistake; and the bus quivered for a moment at the stop, and through the open windows the summer air was sweet and soft as cashmere too. But it was only for a moment, of course, while people got on and off; and the swoop from the colony of high flats into the old duty roots of the Claggans was comforting, like crawling into your own clarty bed after a night on a hospital cot. There was still a lot of building going on, but not, Mrs Sheehan was certain, so much tearing down, as if they were finding it harder going the nearer they came to the stubborn heart of the Claggans. As they turned the corner the last group of tenements stood up like the New York skyline: Sarah Sheehan's house, and Brady's, and Quinn's, it she had known it, and Eugene Garty's, all solid and safe. Even from the top floor you were not too high to see starlings and chimneys. And right enough, the demolition had stopped. Or anyway slowed down.

Her homecoming love had to spill over. In the Pakistani shop at the close-mouth she bought a poke of sweeties. Wee Teresa Lynch never said no to sweeties, and her mother, heavy with her fifth, might like the lemon curd. The Lynches had only come six months ago: it was great to have wee ones around again. Mrs Sheehan tackled the stairs with something like joy. If you did have to walk up, sure God gave you the legs, and nobody else could press a button and take them away from you. Excited herself at the thought of the wee girl's pleasure, she knocked on the Lynches' door.

She knew almost at once that it was going wrong, when they took a long time to answer, and when there was a slap and a wail in the hall. Mrs Lynch, young and toothless, opened the door, easing it with difficulty past her swollen body. Beyond her, in the middle of the hall, wee Teresa, stiff with fury, roared and wept. It wasn't going to go right.

'Oh hullo, Mrs Sheehan.' Mrs Lynch always managed to sound surprised. 'I thought you were away out.'

'Aye, I was-'

In the depths of the Lynches' house a man called, 'Wha' is it, Mary?' Mrs Lynch took no notice; she wouldn't need to, poor lassie, thought Mrs Sheehan, hearing the looseness of drink in the heavy voice. 'I was visiting my married daughter,' she said, 'and I -'

'Mary! Wha' the hell is it?'

'Wheesht, Eddie.' Mrs Lynch contrived to smile in both directions at once; you could see the pretty girl she had been six or seven years ago. Wee Teresa, somewhat recovered, came up and butted into her skirt. She held Mrs Sheehan with an apologetic look while she called over her shoulder, 'It's Mrs Sheehan from upstairs.'

'Christ,' said the drunk voice with dreadful clarity, 'no' that auld bitch again.'

Mrs Lynch, scarlet and miserable, said bravely, 'What did you say you was wanting, hen?' She now looked about wee Teresa's age; Mrs Sheehan's heart was wrung for her. She wanted to say that it didn't matter, not to worry, that she knew the way they went in drink; God, she had a right to. Instead she said, 'I had some sweeties here, I thought wee Teresa might like them.'

'Och, that's awful nice of you, you shouldny,' said Mrs Lynch, almost in tears. 'Come here, Teresa, see what Mrs Sheehan's brung you–'

But it was spoiled for this tune. Mrs Sheehan's hand shook as she brought out the poke of sweeties: wee Teresa, dirty and still whimpering, grabbed them. 'Mary! Whit the hell–' came a roar from the house. Mrs Sheehan said hurriedly, 'I'd better away up and make my tea.'

'Oh my God,' said Mrs Lynch, stopping with the door half shut on her bulk. 'I near forgot, Mrs Sheehan. There was a wumman looking for you.'

Mrs Sheehan paused, puzzled. 'I don't know who that would be. Was it Mrs, Boyle from the UCM?'

'I never seen her,' said the distracted Mrs Lynch. A small brother had appeared on all fours beside wee Teresa and was trying to pull himself up by the hem of his mother's apron. 'I heard your bell, but I was wiping up this dirty wee bugger, I couldny go. She must have rang at the Bradys' then. I heard her talkin' to young Danny.'

'She's away then?'

'I couldny say,' said Mrs Lynch. A shadow appeared in the hall behind her; simultaneously the small Joseph discovered the sweeties and Teresa whipped them up her jersey. Mrs Sheehan said hastily, 'Thanks anyway,' and stepped back. The door closed on the rising tide of roars. Mrs Sheehan went slowly upstairs. Standing, even for those few minutes, had brought on the ache low in her back; her knees she hardly noticed any more. Every time she climbed the stair; much worse, every time she got down on them to scrub; what use, she demanded rebelliously, would I be in the high flats? But the answer was: That's what the lift is there for.

She stopped on the landing to look for her key. That was another change; but why did she have to think of it now? It was years and years since the Sheehans' door had been the ever-open one on the stair, not by plan really, just because people were always running in and out. It never had a chance to shut. Was it really years since little dark thin Bernie had been tearing in and out with her pal Kathleen, who was a novice now in Dublin, and Kieron Brady across the landing, and wee Danny tottering after them with his broad gappy grin? And before Bernie there had been Annie courting her James, and Mary Flora with her big Canadian; and before them the wee boy Michael, God be good to him; it would be thirty years in November since the meningitis. And long before that, the young Peter and Sarah, shutting the door behind them for once and running downstairs to the dancing. And God help me, thought Mrs Sheehan, for she knew now what had set her thoughts on this tack. That poor idiot Eddie Lynch, roaring drunk at halfpast five of a Saturday afternoon.

Well, a quiet house was better than that. Wasn't it? Surely it was. Mrs Sheehan found her key, under the twice-forgotten jar of lemon curd, and turned it in the lock.

The house was quiet enough, certainly. The kitchen faced north: even on this summer evening it was half dark, with the damp coldness that had seeped through the whole building since the roof went in the big gale. It looked over the grim back-court with the crumbling midden and washhouse to the dead windows of another condemned tenement. She was fresh from Annie's bright, modern, sunny kitchen in the sky; she looked through Annie's eyes and saw a dirty slum.

Yet it always had been dark, even in the old days. The back-court and the cliff of tenement had always been there. There was not much furniture, but there never had been: long ago, at New Year and Hallowe'en, people had always ended up sitting on the floor and on each other's knees. It had always been a grey, damp room. Only then you couldn't see the room for people.

And now it was dirty too. She put her shopping-bag on the table: the oilcloth was sticky with dirt, worn through in places. Time was when that would never have been allowed to stay there. How long was it since she had got a new bit of oilcloth for the table, strong-smelling and glossy, or an armful of the cheapest daffodil buds for the window recess? How long since she had even washed the curtains, or rubbed up the grate, or tidied out the press? Twelve months since Peter died. But the house had begun to die before that, six months before, when Bernie went away.

She shivered, a hard long shiver that frightened her a bit: it wouldn't do to take the flu and be lying here with nobody knowing.

(That was the biggest change of all. Never, in the crowded old days, could you have missed even a trip to the midden without somebody wondering if you were ill. But Mary Lynch had her hands full downstairs, and God help you if you had to depend on poor Pat Brady.) June or no June, it was a night for a fire. She knelt by the grate: from the habit of years the sticks and paper were lightly heaped, ready for the match. The miserable little voice that had been her companion in these months told her what an extravagance it was, a fire in midsummer. A widow woman? With just her pension to keep her, when she got too stiff to clean? Now was the time to be saving.

But 'What the hell am I saving for,' said Mrs Sheehan, 'other folk's weans?' and the knots of twisted newspaper blazed up, one, two, three.

The fire caught and held: she was setting the small lumps of coal cunningly among the new flames when she heard the knock at the door. She called come in, forgetting that nowadays, if you believed the papers, it could be nothing better than an axe murderer.

But it was only Danny Brady. 'Mrs Sheehan?' Danny was a nice big lad now, tall for fourteen, with floppy tow hair and still a wee boy's softness about the big eyes and ears. 'Mrs Sheehan, there's somebody to see you.' 'Where? In your place, Danny?'

'Aye, Mrs Sheehan. I asked them in to wait.' Danny blinked and smiled. 'Would you like to come in?'

Mrs Sheehan got slowly to her feet, partly because of her knees, but more to spin out the time of hope in case she was wrong. But she knew all the time. She hardly needed to look past Danny's bony shoulder into the Bradys' airless, smelly kitchen to see the thin dark girl perched on the dirty chair. She saw with no surprise, because it looked so natural, the round pink baby cuddled on Bernie's knee.

'Hullo, Ma,' said Bernie.

'Hullo, hen,' said Mrs Sheehan, while her heart began to thud great thumps of joy.

7

Latecomers, Eugene thought, surely must imagine it was a drunk sailor in the box back from the China run. She had been in there five minutes already—no, nearer ten, and that with Father O'Connor, popularly known as Speedy Gonzales. Eugene, his hands over his face, bled inwardly in his awareness of the lengthening queue behind him, while his mother, in the toneless loud voice of the deaf, confessed her sins to almighty God, blessed Mary ever virgin, all the saints, Father O'Connor, and seventeen Saturday-night penitents.

Not, thank God, that you could really hear what she was saying; only the rhythm of it, the quick rattle of 'Bless me, Father,' the cadences of the *Confiteor* which she always said however long the queue, then the interminable loud murmur. Of course it wasn't possible. She went to confession every week, as he had cause enough to know, and between times she never left the house except on his arm to Mass, devotions, and Tuesday novena. Suppose she sat at home filling every waking moment with blasphemies, it still wouldn't take her fifteen minutes to confess it ...

But she was finished: there was the pattered act of contrition, in counterpoint with the richer voice of the priest; she would be out, he was next, and, God, he wasn't prepared at all. Oh, God, let's see, the usual, lack of charity (thinking about your mother like that, at such a time too) and distractions in church, for distracted he certainly was. His mother came out of the box, leaning heavily on her stick, and he jumped up to help her into a pew near the Lady Altar. He had hoped the schoolgirl next in line would slip in before him, but she, good child, was waiting, letting him have his turn. He scuttled back, thinking of the priest impatient in his stuffy alcove: oh God, charity, distractions, but these were only the little things. Those thoughts, not sin unless you invited them; well then, yes, those thoughts. And the other thing. Could it be counted as thoughts? No, more than that, very well he knew it, and he would confess it, yes, he must. He slipped into the box and went on his knees. Only how to put it, God, that was all.

The first surprise was that it wasn't Father O'Connor.

He knelt on after saying his penance, his elbows hooked over the pew in front, his long white hands loosely linked. He felt drained, as after a mighty effort. But the visiting priest had been understanding: 'Pray to Our Lady,' he had said, 'and I'm sure a little more of the company of other young people would do you no harm.' Of course there wasn't much chance of that. His mother beside him prayed fervently on her clicking beads. Nothing wrong with her hands anyway; there he was again, lack of charity, not five minutes out of the confessional.

Eugene shut his ears to the small sound. He kept his eyes wide open, the haze of light from the candle-stand blurring into the white altar-cloth, all bright against the soft shadows of the unlighted sanctuary. No more of those thoughts, he vowed, even if they do come uninvited. That book, I could surely slip it back into the shop. And that other thing, Lord, I'll never do again.

'Are you not done yet?' croaked his mother, rattling her rosary beads into their pink plastic box. He helped her up and they made an awkward Siamese-twin genuflection in the side aisle. Outside the open door was the Claggans summer evening, warm and dustily sweet. The dirty small children chasing up and down the church steps had rims of gold round their tangled heads.

'Did you put in money?' shouted his mother, so suddenly that he jumped. 'You canny light a candle if you don't put in money.' She was storming at a filthy little girl, no more than three years old, who had been happily lighting candles by the handful and sticking them as high as she could reach on St Anthony's stand. Eugene's mother snatched the latest one from her fat hand and blew it out. The small girl fled roaring.

'I'll pay for her candles,' Eugene said suddenly, surprising himself; but his mother said, 'You'll not be so daft,' and pulled him on. In the backwash of the impulse he did feel rather silly; but at least, he thought, it was a charitable one, it wasn't as bad as those other thoughts. Perhaps Our Lady had sent it to encourage him. Perhaps things were really going to get better.

A crowd of boys and girls came rollicking down the street, long legs and interlaced arms, flopping hair and bright eyes and the flower colours of shirts and dresses. What must it be like to be one of them, laughing and pushing and swearing and cuddling a girl in each arm? No, no use imagining it. In any case they were too young for him. Father couldn't have meant that.

'They're not bound for confession, anyway,' said his mother darkly. 'That's your Catholic youth today.'

Eugene ventured to say, 'I suppose they could be Protestants.'

'I wouldn't be surprised,' said his mother. 'They nearly had us in the gutter.'

The long street from the church took over half an hour to negotiate, moving at a toddler's pace, one foot up to the other. They stopped completely at the corner, and Eugene's mother sat down on the broken wall of the old school, pressing a hand to her uncertain heart.

'It's a pity,' she observed, 'we hadn't a neighbour with the Christian charity to have a cup of tea waiting for us. Did ye mind we were out of tea?'

Eugene said, after the briefest hesitation, 'If you want a rest, Mammy, I could run ahead and put the kettle on -'

'Holy God,' said his mother, 'you forgot the tea.'

'The Pakistani shop stays open late,' said Eugene miserably.

It would need to,' said his mother. 'Have you any money with you?'

'I've a shilling or two,' said Eugene.

'I suppose you gave nothing to the Holy Souls,' his mother said.

The day, thought Eugene as he waited in the busy little shop, had been forty-eight hours long. Only another hour or two before he could get to bed. But what then? He usually read far into the night, library books and magazines, and those other books he picked up in town; but in tonight's mood of honesty he could admit what that led to. No, tonight he would try to get to sleep right away. There might be dreams, but nobody could be expected to do anything about dreams.

In the warm shop with its sharp and sweet and spicy smells he began to drift a little. He became aware of the causeless, dangerous happiness that belonged to the dream, and jerked himself sternly back.

He couldn't have been away for long, though, because he didn't seem to have moved any distance up the queue. He shifted his weight to the other foot and fixed his eye on a pyramid of dog-food cans. When he moved up to the cornflakes stand he would know that he had made some progress.

He stayed with the dog-food. Behind him there began to be a little unrest in the queue. He craned forward to see what was holding things up, and heard for the first time - though he realized now that it had been murmuring on for some minutes - the sweet deep voice of the girl at the head of the queue.

She was saying to the brown-eyed daughter of the shop, 'Sure you're far better up here, Fatima. Some of the houses down in London, I'm telling you, even the rats has up an' left them.'

'Is that right, Bernie?' The pigtailed Fatima hugged to herself a tin of baby milk, in no hurry to finish selling it. 'But is the pay no' better down there?'

'Oh aye,' said the dark-haired girl who was supposed to be buying the milk, 'but the rents is fantastic, mind, Fatima.' Eugene could only see the back of her head beyond two patient customers, and, as one of them shifted his position, a glimpse of her slim shoulders in a cotton dress. She said, 'An' the folk, I don't know. An Englishman's home is his castle, my God, it's mair like Fort Knox.'

'That's what ma blither say,' put in Mr Mohammed, abandoning the deep-freeze to lean on the counter too. 'He say down there where he is, you maybe some kind o' pest they trying to get rid o'. Lucky where you are, Hamid, he aye telling me.'

'Nae place like the Claggans,' said the dark-haired girl. 'Great to be back. Thanks then, see you, Fatima.'

She picked up the tin of milk and whirled away from the counter, grinning at the waiting queue and nodding back at her childhood pal Fatima Mohammed; so that it was no great wonder she bumped heavily into the dream-drugged Eugene.

He started and muttered sorry, and she fell back with a laugh. In the crowded little shop the impact had jolted everybody one place forward or back. She wriggled past Eugene to reach the door, glancing up from long green eyes. She put a hand up to smooth back her dark hair, and he got a breath of lemony perfume from the soft crown of her head. She gave him a little smile, no more than a quiver of the lips. The dusty summer light behind her printed her for a moment, a slight shape against the pink-lit grey stone street.

'Did ye go to Ceylon for it?' his mother wanted to know.

8

Bernie, whose glance and smile had been as unthinking as a sneeze, came out happily with her tin of milk. She was glad to be back in the Claggans. She had missed in London, without knowing it, odd things like the long light evenings, and people to nod to, and Pakis with broad easygoing Claggans voices. The air, warm as it was, struck sharp after London air. Her delicate face was pink with its freshness and her eyes were bright as a little cat's as she turned into her close. At the same moment a young man turned into it from the opposite direction.

'What are you laughing at?' he said when he had his breath back; then, looking more closely at her, 'To hell, it's Bernie Sheehan.'

'Kieron Brady,' said Bernie, and laughed still more. 'Only you're the second fella I've knocked kicking in five minutes.'

'You haveny changed a bit,' said Kieron. He leaned one hand on the wall above her head and looked down at her: he was nearly a foot taller. 'Mind you, you have, a wee bit. My God, it must be five years since I seen you. Where've you been?'

'I hivny been nowhere,' said Bernie indignantly; for the moment she really believed it. 'It was you that went on the boats.'

'So I did. I came home though when Mammy was bad,' said Kieron. He hesitated. 'You'd know—'

'Aye,' whispered Bernie. 'My mammy told me.' Like a remembered sickness it came back to her, that news and Danny's big eyes filling up with tears, and the terrible, dirty flat without a woman. Suddenly she was tired, too, with the creeping tiredness of the long journey. The pretty colour had all gone from her face, and Kieron stooping over her thought she was going to cry.

'But never mind,' he said hastily. 'Are you home for a while, Bernie?'

'I'm home for good, Kieron,' she said. She became aware of the tin of milk, clutched so tightly as almost to cut her hand. 'I'd better get in,' she said, 'Mammy's waiting for this,' and though her face was white, the sparkle was back in her green eyes. There had always been a quirk beside her mouth, nothing so soft as a dimple, and it was there now as cheeky as when she was fourteen. She looked about fourteen to Kieron. No, that was a lie. She looked nothing of the sort.

"I'll get you up the stair anyway,' he said. 'Do you know is the old fella in?'

'He wasn't before,' said Bernie. 'But Danny's in with my mammy and the baby.' He jumped a little, and no wonder; she'd forgotten for a minute there herself. 'Wee John,' she said. Kieron said nothing. 'His daddy's at sea,' she said. 'I don't think I'll be seeing him again.' Kieron still said nothing, but then there wasn't much to say.

'You took your time,' said Mrs Sheehan comfortably. Wee John was propped against her stomach as she sat, knees apart, in the big old armchair. Danny was sitting on the rag rug at her feet. It was just twilight now, and the low red fire in the range flickered on Danny's big shiny nose and the baby's silky crest of hair.

'I met Kieron in the close,' said Bernie. Kieron said, 'Hullo, Mrs Sheehan.'

'Kieron,' said Danny, 'this is Bernie's baby.'

'I know,' said Kieron with a grin. He put out a long finger and poked wee John, saying, 'Hullo, wee fella.' So that seemed to be all right.

Bernie took the tin of milk to the sink and began to measure out a feed. She did not seem at all perturbed about appearing, husbandless, with a baby: and 'Daddy at sea, how are ye,' said Mrs Sheehan to herself. But it wasn't any time to ask awkward questions, not with the solid, damp, warm baby on her lap.

He sat fatly, his round legs dangling, eyeing Danny and Kieron under ridgy, hairless brows. He shone with the downiness of babies. Mary Flora's two in Canada were only snapshot children; when Pauline was a baby, Annie and James had been on a short-lived emigration down south. It was nineteen years since the last soft baby, who had been Bernie, had butted its head into Mrs Sheehan's ready breasts.

'He's a nice wee fella, isn't he?' she said. 'Looks all right to me,' said Kieron. Danny said, 'He's smiling at you, Kieron! He likes you!'

Bernie came over with the baby's bottle. 'He likes you too,' she said to Danny. 'Do you like babies?' Danny grinned and nodded silently. 'Kid on he's your wee brother, then,' said Bernie, and put the bottle into his big red hands.

Mrs Sheehan glanced sideways at Danny. She might not have said that herself, not to a soft young laddie with his mother just three months dead. But Danny was still grinning, almost as gappily as the baby, some teeth lost and others broken in his big mouth. 'I wisht he wis,' he said.

A finger of worry nudged Mrs Sheehan, but she shook it away. Danny was a nice laddie, that was all. Even in the Claggans you didn't have to be a tearaway at fourteen. But God, there he was like a wet-nurse coaxing the teat into the baby's open mouth. Was there not something just a wee bit too soft in him?

Still, Kieron was watching, leaning against the door with his arms folded, laughing; and they didn't come much more normal than Kieron. 'Have you had your tea, Kieron?' she said.

'Not me. Have you, Danny?'

'Not me,' said Danny. 'I was waiting on you and my da.'

'My God,' said Mrs Sheehan, 'we'd better do something about that,' and she began to heave herself to her feet. Bernie leaned over to take wee John, and, as she took the weight of the baby, Kieron steadied her with a hand under her arm.

That was when they heard the limping footsteps on the stairs.

They all stood quite still for a moment, as if they hoped the footsteps would pass the door. Mrs Sheehan said in a hurry, 'See will your da come in too, Danny. It's just eggs and chips, tell him.'

Danny looked at Kieron, and Kieron said, "He'll maybe have a bucket in him by now, Mrs Sheehan.'

'Ah, ask the man in,' said Mrs Sheehan, almost crossly, and as she turned away to the cooker she muttered something that could have been '. . . nothing new.'

But Brady had heard their voices. When Danny opened the

door he was already standing there, holding himself up by the doorpost. 'Are ye there, son? Whaur the hell are ye? Whaur's ma tea?'

'Okay, Da,' said Kieron, going forward. 'Come on home and we'll get your tea.'

Is it you, Kieron?' said Brady, standing straighter and peering into the room. 'Kieron, son, I saw a lassie today would do you fine. Saw her in the liberry.'

That's fine, Da,' said Kieron tensely, trying to free the clutching hand from the doorpost.

'Lovely lassie,' Brady said. His head began to sink on his breast. 'Lovely, bonnie lassie, fair hair like your mammy. Like your mammy used to be.'

'Danny!' barked Kieron. 'Get that bloody kettle on!'

Danny shot past his father and into his own house. He left the door standing open: from the muddle and mess inside it was as if sad grey tendrils curled across the landing to the Sheehans' warm kitchen. Certainly there was a smell.

'Ah, ma wee Kieron,' crooned old Brady. 'Awful like your mammy.'

Kieron had the arm free and hitched it round his neck. 'Sorry about the tea, Mrs Sheehan,' he said. 'I'll see ye, though. See you again, Bernie.' He humped his father across the landing and kicked the door shut behind them.

Mrs Sheehan waited for Bernie to say something. Bernie stood with the baby on her hip, looking at the closed door: the fingers of her free hand were pressed to her lips.

'My God, Mammy,' she said. 'What happened to him?'

Mrs Sheehan looked sideways at her. 'You'd hardly have seen him,' she said, 'when you were a wee girl?'

'No,' said Bernie. 'Sure he was always away. Kieron used to brag his da was a travelling man.'

'He was that, God help him,' Mrs Sheehan said. 'Ten, twelve years it would be, since Danny was a wee shaver.'

Travelling?'

'On the road,' said Mrs Sheehan. 'Sleeping rough. Twelve years, aye, or more.'

Bernie said, 'I never knew that.'

'Why would you?' said Mrs Sheehan. 'Poor Rose never put it about. She just brung up the boys the best she could. She done well, so she did.'

'Aye,' said Bernie thoughtfully, jiggling John on her hip.

'But she wasny well, and she wouldny tell naebody,' Mrs Sheehan said. 'She let the house go, she couldny help it; God, ye saw what like it is now. And still she wouldny let on.' She stared over wee John's duckling head. 'An' that's where I blame maself, Bernie. I shoulda saw what was up. But first she wouldny admit it, an' then—' Her eyes slanted to Bernie's face. 'Then you went away, an' then your da died, an' I don't know, Bernie. I couldny seem to care.'

Bernie said, when the silence had gone on for a bit, 'But when did he come back, then?'

'Holy Thursday,' said Mrs Sheehan. 'After twelve year, wi' the house like a midden, an' the boys as wild as tinks, an' poor Rose on her death-bed, the bold Patrick comes back to stay.'

She gave herself a shake.

'We'd better finish feeding wee John,' she said, 'if there's any heat left in the bottle at all.'

9

It was another hot night. In the Bradys' flat, where the windows were either warped shut or mended with cardboard, there was not a breath of air. But Kieron and Danny slept soundly in the big bed, because they were young and had had a tiring time getting the boots off the old fella. In the set-in bed in the room old Pat slept heavily too, his toothless mouth wide open and snoring, lapped in the sour smell of neglect.

His snores came through the wall to the Sheehans' house, and Mrs Sheehan heard them because she was lying awake. She did not want to go to sleep and end the day that had brought Bernie back. Instead she began to plan tomorrow: breakfast for three, not just a slice of bread and a cup of tea on the corner of the table; dinner, little enough in the larder, but there was always the Paki shop. The night was warm and happy with Bernie's calm breathing and the soft occasional snuffle from wee John. She would need to see about fitting up the room properly for Bernie, if she was going to stay.

She burrowed into the pillow, thinking about curtains and a rug, and quite unexpectedly she was back in the wee room at the cottage: a corner of left-over space, a tiny window in the camceil roof. The first night she had cried herself to sleep: 'But Sarah, you're getting a big lassie now. You canny sleep a' your days wi' your daddy and mammy.' And after a bit she had loved her wee room. The tears on her first night in a Claggans set-in bed were different, slow hard tears of a girl growing up sooner than she should. She knew that they would only hurt her mother and father, so she hid those guilty tears, and hid far deeper the little queer-shaped room.

And why think of it now, for God's sake? The hills seen from the bus, it seemed to Mrs Sheehan, had opened a door in her mind like the door of a cupboard stuffed too full. Out of the crack slipped tickly bare feet, a camceil roof, a swinging milk-scented udder at the level of two-year-old eyes. What in the world would be next? She fell asleep quickly, as it she had been walking in the blue hill air.

Eugene's mother, who seldom closed an eye all night, was sound asleep. Eugene was awake. He had kept off the books all evening; he had gone to bed early, his mind shriven, empty and pure. The thoughts, the writhing dreams had begun to move in on soft feet. He had pushed them away; and into their place had slipped the girl in the shop, soft hair, green eyes, shy smile. Biddy? No. Betty? No, no. He hunted for her name with no success, and left it to come of its own accord. But she was a real girl, that made all the difference. Not a page from a dirty book: a real, beautiful girl. And she must live somewhere in the Claggans. Eugene, lying on his back, flung one arm over his eyes and began the difficult journey to sleep,

Quinn was not in a mood for reading either. He lay on his bed in shirt and trousers, hands under his head. His top-floor room was as tidy as a ship's cabin: tidier, with no photographs on the dresser, no letters behind the clock. Letters and photographs meant people, and people were not necessary to Quinn. His blue eyes hardly blinked; he was thinking of nothing in particular, heavily content. People intruded, people imposed, probing with questions into your life, telling you what to do. Sometimes the irritation grew too much, and you had to take steps then. He had done everything neatly and well: it gave him pleasure, that sleepy thought. He did not worry about having made any mistakes, because that sort of thing didn't happen to Quinn. The square of sky in his high small window shaded from turquoise to deep blue to black, and a star or two pricked through.

In her pretty bedroom in a council house on the respectable side of the park, Lisa ran her hands through and through her long fair hair. The magazine propped on her dressing-table was open at a double-page spread of new summer hairdos. She plaited, coiled, tied, looped; she swirled the soft heavy hair up on her head and let it fall again in sexy curtains. It was too hot to sleep, and too early besides. It was a lovely summer night, a night to be strolling home with somebody in the long, long twilight under the young scented trees. After tea she had gone down to the bowling-green with her father, and they had been home by half-past nine.

And what chance was there (thought Lisa, who was nineteen) when you worked in a library? Especially Claggans library. She thought of old Brady, and giggled through a mouthful of hairgrips. She thought of Eugene Carty, and shuddered, as any right-minded girl would shudder at a person like that.

But then there was Quinn. Yes, Quinn. She rubbed her cheek, smiling into the mirror, against the fluffy collar of her housecoat, and remembered the direct stare of his sky-blue eyes. She sighed, and shook down her hair, and went to bed.

And quite across the city it was a lovely evening too, in the calm wide avenues and crescents riding high among old trees in a certainty of grey Victorian stone. The little room had once been a maid's bedroom, hot and stuffy for a douce modest girl up under the eaves with the window shut; now it was Helen's study-bedroom, and she had flung open the window and switched her fan-heater to blow cold. She sat on a pouffe, blonde hair curtaining the eager line of her young face, and sang to her guitar 'Plaisir d'Amour'.

'That's as good as what's her name, French one,' said her dark friend Janet admiringly from the floor.

'Will it do, d'you think?' Helen said, thumbing the strings. 'I thought I'd better put in the verse in English for them.'

'It's not long enough anyway,' said Janet, 'for them to start getting bored.'

'And tearing up the seats?' said Helen. Janet blushed, because that was just what she had meant: Helen was so quick in the uptake, sitting there like an elf in her scarlet shirt and trousers, ankles crossed and guitar on her knees. She said, 'Prejudice again, I guess.'

'Yes, Janet, watch it,' said Helen with a giggle. 'Some of my best friends live in the Claggans, you know.' Janet knew enough by now to laugh at that. Helen leaned over, found her piece of paper on the floor, and wrote on it decisively. "Then the boys will do "The Holy Ground" and that will be the first half.'

'It's a pity the boys are away this week,' Janet said, worry corrugating her plain brow. 'What if we fix a date and then they have something else on?'

'They won't,' said Helen. And Janet knew they wouldn't; not if Helen said not. She looked at the bright firecracker face above the idly thrumming guitar, and wondered once more how it felt to be Helen; and then with a spasm of the stomach wondered what they were all thinking of, going down into the dreaded slums of the Claggans with three guitars and a squeeze-box, even for a good cause, even organized by Helen. 'Are you sure,' she said, 'people know about folk-songs down there?'

'Irish and Italians? They're a nest of nightingales,' said Helen. She sounded as if she knew what she was talking about: of course she always did know. Her long fingers teased out the first notes of 'Come Back to Sorrento'. She was the only person Janet knew who could make jokes on a guitar.

There was a quick knock on the door and Helen's mother looked in. 'Working hard, girls? You'll be ready for your supper.' She had brought a big tray with coffee and sandwiches and cherry cake and chocolate biscuits; Janet, stumbling up to take it, found she had pins and needles excruciatingly in her right leg. She hopped about hissing, while Helen uncurled from the pouffe and stretched out her slim arms for the tray.

'Oh Mum, that's fabulous,' she said. 'You shouldn't have, we'd have come down.'

'At midnight, I know,' said her mother fondly, 'and left the fridge door open.' There was a lacy traycloth. There were even paper napkins, filigree in pink and white. Janet leaned heavily on the window-sill, kneading the solid calf of her leg.

Behind her Helen said, "The programme's half done, we'll be able to see the minister and fix a date any time, Mum, don't you think we're clever?' The chestnut tree outside, older than the house, moved gently in its summer sleep.

It was another hot night; even hotter than the night before, when Frances Callaghan had died.

Sunday

1

Kieron sat on the edge of the bed, yawning painfully and scratching both hands through his black hair, for quite five minutes, until Danny, anxious as a housewife, scrambled out behind him and ran in his shirt-tail to light the gas under the kettle. Kieron groaned, hit out lightly at Danny's passing ear, and began to look for his trousers. By the time he had dragged them on and was tipping a palmful of tea into the blackened pot, Danny had put six slices of bread on a cracked plate and brought margarine and jam from the wall press. 'Sit in, Kieron,' he said.

'Right, sit in yourself,' said Kieron. 'You've to get to Mass, boy.'

'Are you not coming?' Danny was alarmed.

'I'm hardly ready,' said Kieron mildly. 'You've got your shirt on at least.'

'Yours is here.' Danny launched himself from the table and scrabbled under the bed. 'And your shoes, they're in the grate.' He ran his sleeve over their cracked toes and placed them invitingly at Kieron's bare feet.

Kieron ran a thumb over his dark-stubbled chin. Danny's big mouth turned down like a two-year-old's.

'I would awful like to go with you, Kieron,' he said.

'Ah, you're a blasted nuisance,' said Kieron. 'Throw me that shirt and drink your tea.'

'All right, Kieron,' said Danny, aglow with delight. 'What about my da?'

'Is he still sleeping?'

'I'll go and see,' said Danny, poised to dart again.

'You'll hell as like,' said Kieron. 'Get that piece and jam down you or you're coming nowhere with me.' He pulled the dirty blue shirt over his head and padded, zipping up his trousers as he went, into the front room. 'Are you wakened, Da?' he said.

Through the grimy windows the sunlight laid a fretted pattern across the room, but it did not reach the set-in bed. Brady slept on his back among the tangled grey blankets. The fallen-in jaws with their coarse grey bristle moved in and out almost imperceptibly to his whistling breath. He stirred, as if he felt Kieron's eyes on him, and muttered in his sleep. The skinny hand lying on top of the blankets flexed and closed on God knew what, and 'Rose,' his toothless mouth mumbled. 'Ah, Rose.'

Kieron turned away quickly. 'Better leave him some bread and jam,' he said.

When they came out of church the first of the day's heat rose into their faces. The tar was already sticky on the roads; the sky was brazen blue. People waiting to get in to last Mass were in summer dresses and shirtsleeves. Danny stopped on the corner and turned his face, with closed eyes, up to the sun. The strings of his thin neck stood out.

'See you at the Gogo after, Kieron,' yelled one of his friends going into church. Kieron nodded, looking at Danny and biting his thumbnail,

'It's gonny be a scorcher, eh, son?' said a comfortable voice behind them.

Mrs Sheehan was straining at the buttons of a wildly flowered house-dress; Bernie was slim as a switch in a scrap of green cotton. The baby sat up in Bernie's arms and beamed around. They made a little knot of happiness in the sunshine. Danny, opening his eyes, grinned wordlessly and went over to stroke the baby's arm with a rough forefinger.

'You're early on the go, Mrs Sheehan,' Kieron said. Danny was still beaming: gone for the moment was the anxious look he had worn ever since, in the Sheehans' warm kitchen, they had heard the old fella's foot on the stair.

'Ah, you haveny much chance to sleep in,' said Mrs Sheehan, 'when there's a wean in the house.' If Danny was smiling, she was blissful: she shifted the heavy shopping-basket on her arm and puffed slightly in the heat. 'We're away down to my good-sister's to see can we borrow a pram. Her Bella's wee Gerard's running about. Then we're away to make the best of the day.' She saw Danny, like the big soft lump he was, still rapt in the baby, and Kieron with a line between his brows still looking at Danny. God love the boys, Kieron all unshaved and Danny with a dirty jammy face, they were a holy show for a Sunday morning. 'Where are you off to yourselves, then?' she said.

Kieron hunched his shoulders. 'The fellas get together down at the Gogo,' he said. 'But this tinker here, I don't know what the hell he does like, but he disny like the Gogo.'

Danny looked up with a brilliant smile. 'It stinks o' sweaty feet,' he explained.

'You're no' far wrong at that,' said Mrs Sheehan. 'Are ye coming with us, then? We're away to the park to give wee John his airing.'

'We've got plenty with us for dinner,' said Bernie, speaking for the first time. Her wide innocent eyes swept both Danny and Kieron in their green glance. 'We'll not be back till tea.'

'Kieron?' said Danny tentatively.

'You an' your sweaty feet,' said Kieron. 'I've to meet the fellas at the Gogo. You go with Mrs Sheehan, and behave yourself or I'll rattle the ears off you.'

'Aw, Kieron, you're a toff,' said Danny in ecstasy.

'And come here a minute.' They conferred, Kieron issuing stern instructions and Danny earnestly nodding and shaking his head, while Mrs Sheehan rocked on her heels and beamed at Bernie.

'I'm no' as daft as I look,' she said. 'Danny will carry the basket.'

Bernie was looking at Kieron. 'What about their da?'

'What about him?' said Mrs Sheehan tartly.

'Well, his dinner.'

'He'll not starve,' said Mrs Sheehan. 'We'll all be back by tea-time. And you'll not bother mentioning him this afternoon, Bernadette.'

'He's their da after all,' said Bernie, a little affronted.

'Just that,' said Mrs Sheehan. 'And I'm thinking they're entitled to a day off.'

Kieron gave them a wave and loped off down the street to join a crowd of young men sauntering in the direction of the Gogo. Danny ran back to them, his hands clasped like a treasure-bearer.

'He gi'ed me half a dollar,' he announced.

'Well, now,' said Mrs Sheehan, 'it's you that's in luck today.'

'It's to buy ice-cream for you and Bernie,' said Danny in the very accents of Kieron. 'But not for wee John unless his mammy says so, or he'll put his boot up—'

'We'll try wee John with a drop on the edge of a wafer,' said Bernie hastily. 'If he's sick you can tell Kieron it was my fault.'

'He only says that,' Danny explained. 'He wouldny really —'

Mrs Sheehan plumped her shopping-basket into Danny's arms and took the gurgling baby from Bernie. They passed along the street lightly, laughing in the sunshine. Bernie swung her arms, cramped from the baby's soft weight, and skipped ahead like a schoolgirl, so that Eugene Carty, sitting reading by his window, looked up and saw her alone. She had tied her dark hair back with a green ribbon: the little green dress skimmed her small breasts and hips; her arms and legs were slender and bare. Eugene, when she had passed, took his hand away from his mouth and stared at the toothmarks on the knuckles.

2

Quinn, lying on his favourite patch of grass up near the flagpole, read a page here and there, with little interest, in his Sunday paper: then he took off his executive hornrimmed glasses and rubbed the bridge of his nose, as if resting his eyes. He was long-sighted. When he looked up, the whole park lay before him in exquisite detail, as if drawn by a mapping pen. The precision appealed to him, for he lived neatly most of the time, obeying private rules as well ordered as the dance of the sun and moon. But there was a more amusing side to it. He had long ago realized that when you took off your glasses people thought you ceased to see clearly.

So they had no idea he was watching them: the long-legged schoolgirls on the roller-skating rink, the student nurses sprawled over their textbooks, the boys and girls sauntering under the dusty trees. He might just as well have had binoculars. The turn of a head down by the river came clearly to him: the movement of a boy's hand, the girl's pettish or co-operative response.

It was all so clear to him; what they were doing and saying; even what they were thinking. There was a sodden old tramp pacing out the time till his next jag of meth. There was a picnic party, one of scores on the trodden lawns. A fat old woman in a sweat-darkened print dress, a half-naked baby, a lumbering adolescent lout with adenoidal mouth ajar; and a girl in a green frock so skimpy you could see her breasts and backside; but she was a skinny black-haired thing, not worth wasting time over. He lay back and let his careful eyes move over the crowds.

There was a rowdy gang of young men, jumping over outstretched legs, yippeeing and cursing. Alarmed sun-bathers drew in their feet, called back their children; Quinn looked them over coldly with his pale-blue eyes. Uncouth, that was all: they had no power. Some had long hair, some had beards, some both: some, with their pale spotty faces and undershot jaws, would have looked better bearded. Their suits were too tight for a hot day, their shoes too shiny for walking on grass. They took the last few yards of lawn at a lolloping run and sagged against the rail near Quinn, panting exaggeratedly.

One of them, a dark-haired boy in a dirty blue shirt, drew his fist over his unshaved chin and said something which was inaudible to Quinn. His friends were audible enough.

'Aw God, he's to get shaved. What's your hurry, Kieron? Gonny see your tart? Aw, Kieron's gonny—'

Kieron's reply was concisely filthy. An elderly woman on the bench beside Quinn drew in her breath in a disapproving hiss: the boys were on to it immediately.

'Haw, Kieron, you offendit that wumman. Aw, she's faintit. What a way for to talk, Kieron Brady. You're a bad bugger, so ye are—'

Kieron, laughing, slung a long leg over the park railing and jumped down outside. Hands in pockets, he strolled away in the direction of the docks; his friends, with further obscene and effusive apologies, skylarked off deeper into the park. The woman released her pursed lips sufficiently to say, 'Scruff.'

Quinn, who had returned to his paper, removed his glasses again and gave her his hesitant, rather charming smile.

'Scum of the gutter,' amplified the woman. She looked hard at him and was satisfied: sports jacket and flannels, short thick blond hair brushed back, good Sunday paper. 'It's a disgrace,' she said. 'You're not safe in broad daylight those days.'

'If you believed all you read in the papers,' said Quinn courteously, 'you'ld never go out at all.' She was going to be a bore. He folded the glasses into his pocket and let his clear eyes rove.

'You've got to believe it,' said the woman in some indignation, 'when it's true! You're not going to tell me they made it up about that poor girl from the cafe?'

But Quinn had stopped listening. The flagpole on the hill above was ringed by a railing the right height to lean on: from there you got a good view over the park, though not into people's minds and souls, unless you were Quinn. A girl was leaning on the railing now. She was a goddess. She was tall and fair and wore a brief white dress like a Greek boy's tunic. Her hair was down for Sunday, caught into a long tail over one shoulder. On weekdays she wore it up. On weekdays she was the new girl in the library.

'—murdered in our beds,' the woman beside him was persisting. Quinn nodded and smiled absently.

'Shut up, you cow,' he said.

The woman snapped her head back, incredulous. She got up as abruptly as if he had hit her and walked quickly away. Quinn looked after her, his brow furrowed. He realized that he must have spoken aloud. He was annoyed with himself. That was the sort of thing he really could not afford to do.

3

Bernie lay on her stomach on the grass playing with wee John. Danny lay beside her, his chin on his fists. He said nothing, but when the baby rolled too near the edge of the rug his large-knuckled hand under the soft fat body nudged it back. Bernie said, 'I was near putting him out for adopting, did you know?'

'Were ye?' said Mrs Sheehan. Hold back, now, her sense told her. Last night, picturing Bernie alone and ill and worried in London, she had cried from the bottom of her heart, 'I wish I'd been with you, my wee lamb,' and cool Bernie had said, 'I managed, Ma.' So that was the way of it. 'You'd hardly know,' she only said, 'what to do for the best.'

'I couldny make up my mind,' Bernie was saying, tickling John's feet till he giggled. 'First of all I said I'd keep him, so they let me take him home. Then I thought it wisny a very good set-up, so I put him for adoption. They gave him to a wife on the waiting list, but I hadny signed nothing, not final. Then after a week or two, ach, I was missing the wee bugger.' She rolled over on her back and held the baby above her at arm's length; he kicked and chuckled ecstatically into her laughing face. 'So I took him back,' she said. She made kissing noises at wee John.

Danny said, 'What did she say?'

'Who?' said Bernie, frowning.

'The wife who thought she'd got a baby,' said Danny.

Bernie looked at him in surprise. 'She only had him on approval, like' she said.

'You'll have that wean spewing up his dinner,' said Mrs Sheehan. Bernie laughed and lowered John on to the rug beside her. She lay relaxed, the baby in the curve of her arm, smiling up into the leafy tree. 'Oh, Ma,' she said, 'this is the life.'

'It'll be awful good for wee John,' said Mrs Sheehan tentatively.

'He's getting a tan already,' crooned Bernie, her long fingers smoothing over the baby's downy cheek.

Mrs Sheehan heaved herself into a more comfortable position against the tree. Still delicately she said, 'Near as good as living in the country,' and held her breath.

'Well, it's no' exactly the Costa Clyde,' said Bernie with a laugh.

'No, it's no', is it?' Mrs Sheehan leaned forward eagerly. Her back gave a terrible twinge: daft she was, of course, getting down this far, God knew how she'd get up again. But this was a good chance to speak. 'Tell you what I was thinking there—'

But Bernie was not listening. Her green eyes were looking at something over Mrs Sheehan's shoulder. A little smile tugged her long mouth. 'Well,' she said, 'look what the wind blew in.'

Kieron said, 'Thought I'd better check up how yez was all

behaving.' He folded his long legs and sat down on the rug beside Danny. He had shaved, and brushed his black hair, and put on a clean shirt. It was even an ironed shirt. The folds were so deeply marked, indeed, that Mrs Sheehan wondered if it had been ironed and put away by poor Rose before she took to her bed those three months ago.

'What did you think we'd be doing?' demanded Bernie, and Kieron said 'How would I know what ideas you might have picked up in London?' Danny was still lying flat with his nose buried in his crossed arms, and his big eyes went from Kieron to Bernie and back: their voices rose and clashed like swords, but he knew, like a puppy, not to be alarmed. Wee John, after his exercise, had fallen into a blissful cat-nap. Mrs Sheehan eased her aching back against the trunk of the tree and thought once more about the country cottage. Because now, with Bernie and the baby—

Around them in the park the white-faced Claggans children screamed and played. Sore red patches flamed on thin shoulder-blades and small dirty necks where they had caught the unaccustomed sun: tears tonight for somebody. It wasn't the life for weans, not at all. And this was the best of it; what about the ten grey months when they played in the filthy cold wet streets?

A gang of little boys scuttered past and the dust rose chokingly like fog. Claggans dust was dirty. Mrs Sheehan laughed at herself, but it was true: the country dust of her childhood had been clean. It was a long way back, the white dust of the farm road soft between wee Sarah's toes as she stumped in her print dress sturdily to school.

Aye, and that was another thing. She laughed again at the thought of school in connection with wee John fat and pink on the rug; but time passed, nothing surer. She saw him five years on, not herded into the sunless yard of a Claggans school, but running brown and barefoot on the moor outside the little school she remembered; and she knew it had to be.

But five hundred pounds? How would she ever come by that kind of money? She might have asked James how you went about it: decent soul, he wouldn't have thought she was trying to touch him. Not that James would have five hundred pounds. Not James, nor anybody else she knew. She couldn't lay her hands on fifty herself, and she wasn't the worst off. Kieron in his one clean shirt, with the old man and the boy on his back, wouldn't be able to raise five; Bernie, not fivepence. Suddenly she had the queerest mind-picture of herself, fat and hot, propped against a tree in Claggans Park. How would an old wife like that get five hundred pounds?

Kieron was eating a cheese roll as if it was his first sight of food for a month. Bernie bent over the shopping-bag to search for a cup, and Kieron stopped chewing. Mrs Sheehan's lips tightened for a moment. You saw the wee boys running about the back-courts, you saw them leaving school and starting work; it was easy to miss seeing them as men. Bernie's scoop-necked dress fell away from her breasts as she stooped, and Kieron had every right to look the way he did.

'Danny,' said Bernie, straightening up, 'would you rinse that under the tap there?'

Danny obediently took the cup to the stand-pipe. 'I thought my da was in his bed,' he observed when he came back.

'He was up when I went back to get shaved,' said Kieron. 'God alone kens where he's away to now.'

'I ken too,' said Danny, giggling in delicious blasphemy. 'He's up there talking to a wumman.'

'What wumman?' said Kieron sharply. He rolled over on his elbow and stared where Danny pointed. Brady was by the flagpole with a young blonde girl. He was leaning forward, peering and muttering at the girl; she was pressed back against the railing,t errified, and no wonder.

Kieron was up on one knee. 'Did you ever get that ice-cream, Danny?' he said.

'No' yet, Kieron.'

'Well, what the hell are you waiting for?'

'All right,' said Danny blinking. 'Will I get one for my da too?'

'Aye, you'd better,' said Kieron, 'it might cool him off,' and as Danny turned away, he launched himself up the grassy slope to the flagpole.

Brady was saying 'Rose, ma wee Rose.' His reeking breath hit the girl's face: he put out a shaking hand and she desperately jerked away. A little to the side, where the girl could not see him, a stocky fair-haired young man in a sports jacket was standing, arms folded, watching with interest. As Kieron, panting, reached the top of the hill, the fair-haired man sauntered forward, saying loudly 'Is he bothering you, miss?'

Kieron took his father by the shoulders and yanked. The old man was light as a dried bone: he came spinning away from the girl and collapsed on hands and knees against the railing. Kieron said, 'I'm sorry, missis. It's all right, Mac. He's drunk. I'll look after him.'

'Look after him?' said the young man sharply. 'The police ought to look after him. I saw him trying to —'

Even in the confusion of the moment, what passed through Kieron's mind was 'And damn all ye did about it.' He said only, 'No, no. He disny know what he's doing when he's like this.'

'Then he should be locked up—' the young man began, but the girl said, 'It's all right. Thanks. Never mind.' She bit her lips and took a deep breath, and she had a fine body under the clinging white shift. The young man said to her, 'Excuse me, miss, but you're in the library, aren't you?' and she smiled and said 'That's right, I've seen you there —' Kieron forgot about them. He turned to his father.

'You old bastard,' he said. 'I ought to kick the tripes outa you. What's the idea?'

Brady knelt in the red gravel and raised his shaking hands to his face. 'Rose,' he said. 'Rose.'

'Ah, God,' Kieron said. He went down on his knees beside the old man. 'Are you listening, Da? Did you hear what that fella said? They'll lock you up if you do things like that.'

Brady's brimming eyes stared from behind his dirty fingertips. 'I thought it was your mammy, son,' he said.

Kieron said desperately, 'It couldny be my mammy.' Sweat was pouring down his back, not from the heat of the day. 'Da,' he said, 'my mammy's dead.'

Brady clasped his hands over his head and rocked to and fro. 'Rose,' he said, 'where are ye, Rose?'

Kieron felt a touch on his shoulder. Mrs Sheehan was panting from the climb to the flagpole, her vast dress clung to her breasts and belly: she was a dark pillar against the sun. 'He's in the horrors, Mrs Sheehan,' he said.

'Aye, so I see,' said Mrs Sheehan comfortingly. 'Come on, Pat. Let's get you to your bed.'

'Rose,' moaned Brady, Mrs Sheehan said, 'Aye, all right, Pat. Rose wouldny like to see you like this.'

They got his arms round their shoulders and walked him fairly steadily down the hill. There was a gate nearby: out in the leafy side street, away from the interested eyes in the park, Kieron blew out his cheeks and said 'Where's Danny?'

'Danny's all right,' said Mrs Sheehan. 'He's bought ice-cream for Bernie and wee John. And if the baby's sick on it we all ken where you'll put your boot.'

Kieron gave something between a laugh and a sob. 'What are we to do with this old bugger?' he said.

'I didny know he was as bad as this, Kieron.'

'He's been awful quiet since my mammy died,' said Kieron, taking a fresh grip on Brady's limp arm. 'He's aye took a bucket, but my God, he's surely on the wine now. Or the meth. I never seen him this bad.'

'Who's this lassie he was pestering?'

'Christ knows,' said Kieron. 'He thinks she's my mammy. Mrs Sheehan, he'll get himself run in.'

They reached the corner where the old school stood, and lowered Brady to a seat on the wall. Mrs Sheehan sank down beside him, legs apart, and breathed in great gulps of air. Kieron sat on the other side, propping his father up. His white shirt stuck to him, dark with sweat, and his hair was plastered over his forehead.

'You looked awfy smart half an hour ago, Kieron,' said Mrs Sheehan regretfully.

Kieron began to laugh in painful gusts like hiccups. He put his hands up to his face and rocked back and forward on the wall.

'Oh, son,' said Mrs Sheehan in alarm, 'don't go hysterical on me."

Kieron made a great effort and clenched his teeth on the laughter. Down the street, moving slowly, came a lame old woman, blue-lipped, leaning heavily on the arm of her son. The pale young man hesitated as they passed, as if he might have offered to help, but his mother's skinny hand clamped on his arm and steered him past the disreputable trio on the wall. Mrs Sheehan was saying encouragingly, 'We've got this far and never met the polis—'

The lame woman, hobbling by, remarked loudly to her blushing son, 'They're never there when they're wanted.'

Kieron threw back his head and exploded in laughter again, but it was real laughter this time, and Mrs Sheehan joined in. They sat and laughed like a pair of idiots, while between them Brady's chin rasped slowly down on to his dirty coat and he began to snore.

'Oh, my God,' said Mrs Sheehan, wiping her eyes. 'We shouldny have let him sit down. Come on, son. He'll be better in his bed.'

They lugged Brady the remaining hundred yards and heaved him into the close. After the sunny park it struck colder than ever, clammy and dark, smelling of cats and worse. Brady was comatose by now. They got him up the stairs and into the house; Mrs Sheehan tossed back the grey blankets; they sat him on the edge of the bed, hauled off his coat, boots and trousers, and rolled him in.

'He'll likely sleep it off,' panted Mrs Sheehan.

'I'm buggered if I know what to do if he disny,' said Kieron. He sat down abruptly on a broken chair beside the table and rubbed his hands over his face.

'He'll be better when he wakes,' said Mrs Sheehan confidently. 'He'll likely sleep round the clock. I'll look in and give him his breakfast, will I?'

Kieron flushed. 'I wouldny want—' he said. 'It's no' very—very tidy in here whiles.'

'Who'd expect miracles from a couple of laddies? You're doing just grand,' said Mrs Sheehan, and saw Kieron's miserable face relax a little. She carefully avoided looking under the table, where they seemed to have stored the garbage of the last three months. 'Now I'm ready for a cup of tea if you're no'. Are you coming in?'

Kieron got to his feet. She thought that he would probably jump out of the window if she suggested it. She said 'Here's Bernie and Danny coming. Sit in the big chair and I'll put the kettle on.'

"Thanks, Mrs Sheehan,' said Kieron hoarsely. He sounded

rather like Danny.

Mrs Sheehan banged the kettle under the tap. 'How in God's name,' she muttered under cover of the running water, 'I could let them get so far through.'

Danny bounced in like a mastiff pup, followed by Bernie with the baby in her arms: his wriggling had pulled up her skimpy skirt to reveal an amazing length of thigh. Mrs Sheehan, glancing at Kieron, saw with love and pity that his tired eyes did not even flicker Bernie's way.

Monday

1

Scarlet, canary, thunder-blue whirled and slashed in the brief summer darkness: Eugene lay on the knife-edge between sleep and waking with his thoughts or his dreams. Wildly and vividly, as so often before, he struggled and panted and thrust and kissed. But for the first time the girl in his mind was a real one, which made it all right. Didn't it? At the very least it meant that there was a chance of making it right.

She had smiled at him out of the dusty sunshine. She was somewhere in the Claggans, slim and white with her tumbling dark hair and strange green eyes. Eugene flung back his head and the night erupted in a rocketing joy of scarlet, canary, blue.

Afterwards there had always, before, been the bitter dust in the mouth, the taste of shame and the dry grey knowledge that it was all invented, all a lie. This time it was different. The colours ebbed and he lay spent and happy, thinking of her. She lived in the Claggans, and he was bound to see her again. God knew where, God knew how he would ever escape from his mother; but the green-eyed girl he would see again.

As the darkness settled around him, he heard a groan from his mother's room.

Her silence was the most terrifying thing about it. Her eyes bulged and she moved her blue lips, but whether in prayer or vituperation he could not tell. The groans were not speech: they came more from her twisted body than from larynx and lips. She was trying to gesture with her clawed hand. Eugene at last caught her meaning and blundered to the bureau, pawing frantically in the clutter of medicines, rosary beads, blessed palms and lavender sachets till he found her drops. His hands shook like blown twigs as he measured and poured.

The drops helped a little, but she was still very bad. She formed the words 'Priest . . .' and 'Doctor . . .' Eugene, as he rushed out to get his trousers, thought he heard her add with her scanty breath, 'Fool.'

Somehow he was in trousers and coat, collar turned up over his pyjama jacket. 'Lie still, Mammy,' he said through chattering teeth. 'I'll be as quick as I can. I'll get the—the doctor — ambulance —'

It was not his imagination this time, the flash of contempt in her piercing old eyes. Her dry mouth fluttered and shaped words again. Quite clearly and impatiently she said 'Priest — first.'

He was out in the dark, breathing street. It was three in the morning. 'Priest,' he said, 'doctor.' Phone for a doctor first, that was only sensible, the doctor would take some time to come; while he was coming, run to the priest's house. He thought hard and placed the nearest phone-box, two streets away. He ran to it, clumsy and hampered by the binding pyjamas under his clothes, and tugged at the heavy door.

The money-box hung askew, hammered in deep gashes. The receiver was gone: the cord, sawn through, ended in a raw stump, shocking as a wound. Eugene bit savagely at his clenched fist.

Where was the next box? There was one beside the Gogo Cafe, but little chance that it was intact down there where the Claggans boys met at night. Surely there was one higher up the hill? Yes, at the corner of the park, near a police box too, so it might be safe.

Eugene began to run again. Half-way up the hill he realized that he was running away from the priest's house, where they might have let him phone; but he ran on. There was not another soul in the sleeping street. Broken walls, jagged cliffs of rubble, the staring sockets of empty windows jolted past him, dreamlike. He panted as he ran.

'What's your hurry, Jimmy?'

The voice and the blinding light hit him like a blow. He flung up an arm and lurched to a stop: a hand closed on his arm, holding him up and holding him back.

'Where d'you think you're away to, eh?'

The two policemen played their torches up and down his shaking body, back along the dark street, the beams fingering up closes and alleys that he had never noticed in his headlong run. His mouth was parched and sore. He gulped and sobbed for words.

'Phone—box,' he said. 'I'm looking for a phone-box. My mother's took ill. Heart attack.'

The torch-beams returned to him, sliding over his drained face and jumbled clothes. He was dimly aware that the pyjamas helped. The beams hesitated and switched aside.

'Where d'you live?'

Eugene croaked out the address. 'The phone's torn out down there. For God's sake let me—'

'Just up there. Take it easy.' The first policeman was an older man, slow-spoken, Highland, not unkind. 'It's an ambulance you'll be wanting. Aye. Go with him, Constable, see he gets through.'

It was the policeman who eventually made the call, when Eugene's cramped fingers fumbled hopelessly round the dial. They saw him back to the house, where in a sudden access of terror he realized that he had forgotten about the priest. But already the ambulance was there, efficient men and stretchers, and a light here and there pricking out to show where, in the half-destroyed tenements, neighbourliness or curiosity still hung on. His mother turned a look of furious contempt on him as she was carried past, but that was nothing new.

Much later that day, in the hospital waiting-room, he picked up a stray paper (his mother thought newspapers a ludicrous Protestant extravagance) and read about the second Claggans murder. He realized at last why the police had been so particularly anxious to pick him up, running for his life in the Claggans night. In his edgy tiredness he could almost have laughed. He was the last man likely to have been murdering a girl late on Friday night. Then and every night that he could remember, the rosary had been said and the chain put on the door by ten o'clock.

'Mr Carty?' said the nurse at the door.

When they had talked kindly and cheerfully to him, he sat down again on the hard hospital chair and smoothed his palms nervously over his sleek black hair. She was pretty bad. She would get better. She would be in hospital for weeks. He pressed his hands together and bit his fingertips. Tonight he would be at home alone.

It was freedom. It was what he had wished for, yes, and prayed for. Eugene ground the heels of his hands against his closed eyes and the dark whirled in scarlet sparks. She was in a hospital bed. What had put her there; or who?

Slim and cool in the chaos of his crowded mind stood, smiling, the green-eyed girl.

2

The first thing Mrs Sheehan knew was the arthritis, nagging at hip-joint and spine. She had laid a mattress on the floor to let Bernie and John have the big bed: that and sitting on the grass in the park, God, she ought to have more sense. And Monday morning, Mrs Devine over in Pollokshields with her stone-floored kitchen: lino over it, but just as hard on the knees. The sun was already up, its early warmth lying across her in great generous bars. It helped a little, and, slipping her hands underneath her, she managed to massage the rolling fat of her back.

From down here she had a new view of the kitchen, the old table with its dirty oilcloth, the chairs with the split seats leaking horsehair. The fingering sunbeams were soupy with dust; dust sifted soft and thick on dresser, mantelpiece, window-sill. It wouldn't do, not with wee John here. And where were the ornaments she used to have about the place? The china dog she had given to Annie, though it wasn't to be seen in the new flat. Mary Lynch had admired the cup and saucer from Dunoon, so it was downstairs now, if wee Joseph and Teresa and the rest hadn't done for it long ago. No, it wouldn't do, that. You had to keep the house homely, when it was needed as a home.

Wee John had been twittering and chuckling to himself for some time. Now he gave a more decided cry, and Bernie, turning over in bed, murmured 'Ah, shut up, ye wee tinker.' It was morning. Mrs Sheehan gathered her muscles together and found that she could by no means get up off the floor.

'Bernie, ma flower, would you give us a hand?'

'Hmm?' said Bernie sleepily.

"Give us a pull up, hen. I'm down here to stay else.' She laughed, though it hurt a bit.

Bernie laughed too and bounced out of bed in her fingertip nylon nightie. They clasped hands and Bernie dug her curling toes into the mattress: heave, flurry of blankets, Mrs Sheehan floundered up on to her knees and then to her feet. 'Holy God,' she said. 'It's time I went on that diet right enough.'

'I told you I would sleep down there,' scolded Bernie.

'In that wee goonie? You'd get your death.' Mrs Sheehan reached out to a chair for her corsets. 'Not at all. We'll sort the room for you, that's what we'll do. You could even start when I'm at Mrs Devine's.'

'Aye, sure,' said Bernie, floating round the room on her slim white bare legs.

'Should have got down to it yesterday,' said Mrs Sheehan, 'but och, it was such a great day, we couldny waste it.' She struggled into her clean checked overall and strained the buttons into their holes. 'It was nice in the park, eh, hen? You could take wee John down again today.'

'I might' said Bernie. 'It's another scorcher, going to be.' She tiptoed at the window, peering out over the empty, sunny wilderness of broken stone. 'It would make you want to go down the coast somewhere, this.'

'So it would,' said Mrs Sheehan eagerly. She stood with her stockings in her hand: she began to tremble a little in her excitement. 'Or even if you lived down the coast all the time, or in the country, that would be great, eh?'

'Sure would,' said Bernie, doing press-ups on the edge of the sink.

Mrs Sheehan drew a deep breath. 'Would you like—' she said, and could say no more for a moment. 'Would you like it if we had a wee cottage in the country?'

Bernie dropped back on to the soles of her feet and stared open-mouthed at her mother. 'Oh aye,' she said. 'And a wee yacht down at Rosneath for the week-ends we wereny asked to Balmoral.'

'No, I mean it.' And suddenly it came rushing out, like tears long held back, only this was happiness, purely joy was this. 'We'll need out o' here, you know that, this place is to come down any day. An' I couldny stick the high flats, could you, Bernie, could you? A wee house we could get, just this size, it's a' we'd need. But a garden for John, an' nae stairs, I'm that slow on the stairs getting-'

'Aye, Mammy,' said Bernie, gentle for her. (She thinks I'm daft, thought Mrs Sheehan tolerantly.) 'Only the last time I seen Andrew Carnegie he never spoke to me, I don't know what I done.'

Mrs Sheehan said flat and plain, 'We only need five hundred pound.'

Bernie set her back against the sink, staring still. 'Five hundred pound,' she said.

'Annie's James says so.'

'Well,' said Bernie. She sank down on the mattress, rocking to and fro. 'Ye've only the five hundred to get, then.'

'Aye,' said Mrs Sheehan. She could have cried. Bernie hadn't said anything, but all of a sudden the whole impossibility of the thing came over her. A garden for wee John? Wee John would be married before she had saved five hundred pounds.

Bernie sat up, cross-legged, her eyes dancing. 'You'll just need to go to the bingo, Ma,' she said.

'The bingo!' said Mrs Sheehan in disdain. She paused. Lighted foyers as she hurried back from a late cleaning job; gaudy canopies, notices about snowballs and jackpots: 'The bingo?' she said. 'I never thought o' that.'

'Och, Mammy, where've you been? A good snowball and you're buying your wee house.'

'I couldny, though,' said Mrs Sheehan. 'I couldny go on my own.'

'Who said you would? I was on the crack yesterday with Mary Lynch downstairs. She goes every Tuesday and Thursday.'

'No' just now, surely?'

'Allow her. She says wee Joseph was near as a toucher called Kelly's Eye, an' this one can take its chance too.'

'Maybe I will then,' said Mrs Sheehan. She was almost afraid. Monday today; by tomorrow night, would she— bingo!—have five hundred pounds? Never, surely. Yet people did, sometimes. She walked slowly to the sink and filled the kettle, holding it under the tap till the water splashed over her hand.

'You're a corker, though,' said Bernie on the mattress, shaking her head. 'Gardens an' stairs! How long have ye been working it out, eh?'

'Since you an' wee John came,' said Mrs Sheehan.

'Aw, Mammy, come off it! That was only day before yesterday.'

'Well, right enough —' She could tell Bernie about seeing the blue hills from the bus, but ach, it sounded daft. She only said, 'Mind your granda was a farmhand out by Strathblane. We didny move in till I was near on ten.'

'You musta got used to the country before you knew, like,' said Bernie sagely. Wee John set up a more determined crying: she jumped up, saying 'I'll get his feed mixed. Is this the only other jug you've got, Mammy?'

'Aye, I'm sorry, hen. I smashed the big yin a while ago.'

'Disny matter,' said Bernie cheerfully, tapping wee John on the nose as she passed him.

'Aye, it does, though,' said Mrs Sheehan. 'I couldny be bothered getting anither yin. God help me,' she said, pausing as she set plates on the table. 'Rose Brady let her house go because she was lying wi' her death on her. I've my health, thank God, an' look at the slitter o' a place I've kept.'

'Och, Mammy, it's no' that bad.'

'Mind how I used to be aye getting wee things for the house?' said Mrs Sheehan, running her hand over the dented curve of the teapot.

'Aye on a pay-day,' said Bernie, sparkling to the memory, 'a wee ornament for the mantelpiece or a cloth for the table -'

The doorbell jangled and Bernie jumped and giggled. 'Oh, Mammy, I'm no' dressed. Who will that be at all?'

'A Paki selling nylons, likely. I'll sort him,' said Mrs Sheehan. She went out into the lobby, stepping lightly. There was a strong whiff of the damp mustiness that hung about the whole house those days, kept at bay in the kitchen only by the warm smells of food and fire. She put back her head and sniffed it up defiantly. Not long now. She tried to remember the country smells from when she was a wee girl, but the best she could do was a mixture of the grass in the park and the soft air stroking through the bus window.

She opened the door to a young man with a suitcase. The dampness of the lobby flowed out to meet the chill of the stone landing, and she shivered: God, you'd think the poor fella was the angel of death.

He was a nice polite young man, fair-haired in a blue suit: he had polishes and brushes and washing-up liquid in one side of his case, and bits of ornaments in the other. Mrs Sheehan let him do his patter, though she liked him less as a hint of an Irish accent creamed his tongue. Unless she was much mistaken, not till he saw the rubbed brass nameplate saying SHEEHAN had that brogue been born.

She was about to settle for furniture polish and a toothbrush when Bernie looked over her shoulder: hastily dressed in a cotton frock, she had the baby on her hip and a laugh in her voice. 'Buying something for the cottage, Mammy?'

She doesn't believe me yet, thought Mrs Sheehan calmly. She said, 'Aye, just that. Is that a rag rug you have?'

There was an excitement about shaking out the thin gay rug: how would it go before a cottage fire? 'With a cat,' said Bernie, still half-mocking, and wee John patted a fat hand at the bright colours. She took it, and then saw a round brass kettle in another corner of the big case: just right for primroses, or the little wild roses of midsummer hedges. She knew she couldn't afford it, and bought it too.

'Well, you've done it now,' said Bernie, giggling as she helped to carry the rug into the kitchen. 'You'll need to get a cottage now to put it in.'

'We'll get a cottage,' said Mrs Sheehan. She was quite sure about that.

'Yon salesman found a soft mark here,' said Bernie. 'He'll be back tomorrow with all the junk he canny sell.'

'I wonder will he,' said Mrs Sheehan. As she and Bernie exclaimed and giggled over the rug and kettle, he had stood back, looking down on them, not a smile on his face. Fair enough, he wasny paid to smile; but he looked as it, as if—

'As if he didny like people,' offered Bernie.

Mrs Sheehan shook her head. 'More as if he wasny people,' she said.

3

Quinn had wakened early, as he usually did, in his top-floor room. No one had ever called him lazy. He got up, heated a kettle of water, and shaved, drawing the blade firmly over his fair stubble and smoothing its track with particular fingers. When he was satisfied, he washed and dressed, putting on a clean shirt and his weekday suit, immaculate after its two days on a hanger. His appearance was important to him, and he was pleased with it when he finally stood at the mirror brushing his thick gold hair.

Then the smooth day showed a flaw. He went to the door for milk and found it had not been delivered. He looked on both sides of the doorway, moved yesterday's empty bottle as if it might be hiding a full one, even went a step or two downstairs. His lips tightened. Not good enough, this sort of thing. He hoped it was not a sign for the day: because when Quinn had a bad day, it could be very bad.

But below on the crazy stairway, to the sound of clattering boots, appeared the red head of the cheerful missing milkboy.

'You're very late,' said Quinn.

'Van broke down,' said the boy, crashing the bottle on to the stone step.

'Very well,' said Quinn. 'Don't let it happen again.'

The boy plucked up the empty bottle, grinning inanely: he seemed to take this as a joke. Quinn said sharply, 'You must understand that it's extremely awkward for business people when the milk doesn't arrive in time.'

The boy raised his sandy eyebrows and said in a surprised voice, 'Bugger you, mate.' He cavorted away downstairs; Quinn stood thoughtfully tapping his thumbnail on his teeth. Had he gone a little too far again? Not advisable to overdo it, even with people like that. No, on the whole he thought he had, as usual, put his case very reasonably, and the milkboy was an insolent young lout. He carried the milk indoors.

After this slightly ominous beginning it was a remarkably good day. Remarkably, because his route for the morning lay among the remaining slums of the old Claggans, where out of every ten houses eight were empty and two bug-ridden rat-holes. Not an area where one could expect much custom, even on the humdrum household side of the stock.

Yet he had one good sale, from a fat old woman who exclaimed over his suitcase as if it was a Christmas tree, and then bought a sleazy rayon rug and a mock-brass pot. The rug would fray and the brass peel within three months, but by then she would be rehoused anyway and would long have forgotten his face among a hundred other salesmen. One or two small sales followed, from the few housewives still putting a good face on things in the ruins of the Claggans. When he turned into the public library to write up his books, he was fairly pleased with himself. This morning, at least, nobody had crossed Quinn.

He was a little put out to see, on duty behind the reading-room counter, the young blonde girl from the park. After the episode of the old man they had exchanged a few words; only a few, but more than Quinn usually allowed himself without a very good reason. You could become involved with people that way. It would be a pity if every visit to the library meant that he had to pass the time of day with that great cow.

She looked up as he came in. Not entirely to his surprise, an adolescent blush ran up to her high broad cheekbones and she lowered her eyes again to the pile of books on the counter before her. At first glance she looked a self-possessed big bitch, but see that painful colour and those great hopeful eyes. She wasn't as experienced as she wished she was. My God, Quinn thought, I should have let the old bastard get on with it. (It did occur to him, and he acknowledged the thought with a twitch of a smile, that indeed he had done nothing to prevent it.) Gravely he made his way to his usual table in the corner, and her thick fair eyelashes rose and fell like Venetian blinds.

He began to write up his notes, neatly as always, in pencil at first in case of errors, though he seldom made an error. The reading-room, for once, was quiet. Most of the usual old men were in, but they were reading peacefully, or at least bending over papers and magazines. It was warm; quite soon it grew rather too warm for Quinn.

The smell of the old men had met him thick and solid at the door. He had closed his nostrils to it as best he could, but now it pressed round him like a mouldy blanket, impossible to ignore. A dark-eyed, stooped old man at the next table kept scratching his fingers through his long greasy hair and thoughtfully examining the nails. Nearby a bristly-chinned old tramp —he might have been the one from the park, but they all looked alike to Quinn —began an irregular and noisy sniffing. From his red eyes two tears of rheum or maudlin self-pity made snail-tracks down his filthy face. Quinn frowned and scribbled in his book.

Then Jamie Ratface began to snore. His head was down on the table, his face turned trustfully sideways: there was nothing to muffle the snore, and it was a particularly grating one, beginning in a whistle and ending in a honk. It filled the big room, shredding Quinn's concentration to rags. He gritted his teeth and looked up vexedly at the girl on duty.

She was in trouble. She half-stood up, as if going to cross the room and wake Jamie; then she sat down again, as if unable to nerve herself to touch him. Instead she frowned severely and cleared her throat. A crescendo of snoring totally swamped the tentative sound.

Her easy blush came up again and she began to bang books around the desk, obviously in the hope of waking or at least distracting the snorer. But Jamie had slept, in brickfields and back closes, through far worse than that. The only result was twice as much noise in the reading-room. Quinn was extremely annoyed. He could almost have gone over and shaken the old fool awake himself, but that would have meant getting involved.

The bright dark eyes of the greasy old man took in the situation. 'S a' right, miss,' he called, 'I'll waken him fur ye.' He got up, stumped past Quinn—he smelled like the backyard of a chip-shop — and laid his big dirty hands on the back of the sleeper's chair.

'Wake up, Jamie boy,' he said, most tenderly vibrating the chair. Jamie woke. He gave a wild snort, leaped convulsively like a gaffed fish, and fell off his seat. The crash woke all the other old men, who began to exclaim and cackle and demand what the hell was going on. The girl at the desk sat staring in fascinated horror, and Quinn bent over his notes in a fury of vexation.

Old Moses picked Jamie up, soothed him down, and lumbered back to his place. The commotion gradually settled. Quinn, glancing up crossly, caught a glimpse of the old tramp from the park. He had taken no notice of the goings-on: he was sitting bleakly upright, his hands clasped between his thighs, and the tears were rolling fast down his cheeks.

Old Moses looked sideways at him, hesitated, and decided to let him alone. The old tramp got up and limped across the floor, dragging a leg. The smell from him was indescribable: Quinn covered his face with his hand. Why in God's name were those old wrecks allowed to go on polluting the air? There were places for people like that. He took up his pencil again and began to write with angry little jabs. The pencil-point broke.

That was really annoying, because he did not carry a knife, and his notes were not yet ready for inking in. He thought of packing up and going home; but that would mean he was behind schedule with his work, something Quinn could not bear. He crossed the room to the counter and said as coldly as he knew how, 'Miss, have you a pencil-sharpener there, please?'

She rummaged in a drawer, found one and gave it to him. She also gave him a tentative smile. He carefully sharpened the pencil, leaning over the counter so that the shavings curled accurately into the waste-basket. As he handed back the sharpener, the girl gulped and batted her eyelashes and said in a little fluster, 'I was very rude yesterday. I never thanked you properly.'

'What for?'

'Helping me with that horrible old man.'

Quinn smoothed his pencil-point with a thoughtful forefinger. How amusing. She had decided to believe that he had in fact helped her. Yes, well; he probably would have done something about it sooner or later.

'I didn't like to mention it,' he said.

The girl caught him up eagerly. 'I thought you might think I'd be embarrassed. It was rather a — a horrid experience.'

'I'm sure,' said Quinn politely.

'And the awful thing is,' said the girl, her fair skin flushing once more, 'he comes in here, you know, every day. Well, you saw him just now. I can't even bear to look at him.'

God help you, madam. 'Couldn't you ask for a transfer?'

'Oh dear,' said the girl, half-laughing, 'it's not as bad as that, I suppose. I'll get over it. If only he behaves himself after this.' She opened the drawer to put away the pencil-sharpener. Her smooth young profile, the line of her cheek and the knot of fair hair at her neck, set up a far vibration in Quinn's mind: I have been here before.

She said with downcast eyes, rearranging the books in front of her, 'Of course if I'm lucky I may miss him. I have pretty regular hours on reading-room duty. Eleven to one normally, and again from four to five.'

Indeed, said Quinn, not aloud. Fancy. A *silly* young cow, as well as everything else. Quite a bonus, that, if you had the inclination. And eager to please, clearly; to which Quinn had no objection.

He thanked her civilly and went back to his writing. What he wrote, his blue eyes intent above the feverish scrawl, had nothing to do with orders or sales. When he finally blinked and paused and read through the scribbled pages, he folded them together, his face impassive again, and put them in his brief-case. They would be burned when he got home. In Quinn's position one had to be a little careful about that sort of thing.

4

Eugene left the hospital after evening visiting-hour, walking in a dream. Hospital for two weeks anyway, and then there would be convalescence. 'Is there anybody at home to look after her?' they asked him. 'Daughters? Neighbours?' He stared at them, bewildered, and shook his head. He felt that everyone should know by looking at him, the simple situation: always since he could remember, just his mother and himself.

Nearly everyone had moved by now from the crumbling close; in any case his mother had long ago antagonized all the neighbours. The flat downstairs was tenanted by four or five girls, some of whom always seemed to be at home. But even Eugene recognized that they had business on hand other than nursing a crabbit old woman.

So she was in hospital (put there by what? by whom?) and he walked dazedly down the familiar street. Once for a few inglorious months he had been a boy scout and carried heavy rucksacks on uncomprehended hikes. His feeling now was the one you got when you took off the pack: a light-headed springiness, as if you might hit your head on the sky.

Turning a corner he staggered a little, as if something really had put him off balance like the long-ago rucksack. He thought wisely that he must be hungry. Cups of tea in the hospital, a sandwich at his desk during the few hours he had managed to spend at the office: yes, he needed food. When you thought of eating in the Claggans you thought of the Gogo Cafe.

The famous Gogo was open and busy again, though no busier than before the murder: already the ghouls had moved on to their next port of call. A hand-written notice on the window announced that help was wanted, evenings. The Antonios were business people. They had had a Mass said for Francie Callaghan, and life went on.

The cafe was one long narrow room, thrusting so deep into its half-derelict block that its back door opened on to the cobbled streets and pale lemon lights of the docks. In the far end the tables were packed in just a chair-breadth apart, and there the teenagers congregated. What they did there Antonio did not enquire too closely, except when there were real screams and knives; but they usually went outside for any really serious disagreement. There was hardly room to operate in the back-room of the Gogo.

In the front, near the counter, the tables were more easily spaced and the company more varied. Old men, shift workers, young couples who had moved up from the back-room gang: Eugene hesitated in the doorway before he saw an empty seat, opposite the coffee machine, back to the wall. He ordered sausage, egg and chips and carried it to the table.

Funny how empty an evening could be. He had never had this problem before, never would have believed he could find himself looking for something to do. He was not a drinker. It was too late now for the library. He still had the three books at home, two borrowed and one stolen: but their imagined ecstasies rang hollow, now that he knew the green-eyed girl.

And he knew what he was going to do, in this strangely free evening, in the others, guiltily free, to come. Perhaps he had known from the very first, when he stood looking down at his blue-lipped mother and had to be told how to help her. His knees began to tremble uncontrollably under the table. He had (though how ?) time — two weeks, three weeks?—to find the green-eyed girl.

Yet how could he find her? He only knew that she lived in the Claggans; supposed it, rather, because she had run down to the Pakistani shop without coat or handbag. Two or three weeks might be none too long. He must not waste a minute of it. In the long light Claggans evenings people were about, walking in the streets and the park, talking in doorways. He would walk with them, looking for her. He would start now.

He began to get up, and saw her standing at the counter.

Tongue tipped out in concentration, she was taking an ice-cream wafer from Mrs Antonio and passing it to a lad beside her, probably her young brother. He squeaked and shook his fingers at the cold impact: she laughed and said 'Drop it, that's right.' He remembered the voice, rather deep, warm and exciting as brandy. And kind, surely, sweet and kind. Under the table Eugene's hands gripped convulsively together.

'There you are, Bernie,' said Mrs Antonio, handing over her change. 'You like being home again, eh?'

'Oh, it's great, Mrs Antonio.' It was a real Claggans voice; she was a Claggans girl all right, but bright, fresh, pretty as could be. 'Some weather this, eh? Good weather for ice-cream?'

'Canny complain,' said Mrs Antonio placidly.

'Bet you canny,' said Bernie. 'I'll be living in here if this goes on.'

That'sa goo,' said Mrs Antonio. 'Mind me to your mammy, eh?'

'Sure,' said Bernie, and with the boy at her heels she ran out like a small girl.

Eugene sat frozen in his seat. Leaving his sausage and egg congealing on the table, get up, run after her? Get up, run after her, come back later and finish his eating? He did neither: and the girl and boy crossed the street, going up the hill. But that didn't prove much, since there was nothing down the hill except the docks.

He pulled himself together. This was something after all. He knew her name now, Bernie —Bernice? Bernadette?—and that she lived with her mammy. She was a Claggans girl, who had been away and had come home. She was very young: no wonder he had never noticed her before. If she had been away for any length of time, he must have seen her only as one of the shrieking schoolgirls in the Claggans streets. She was what he wanted and what he needed. He got up in a daze to pay his bill.

Outside the cafe he paused to plan his next move. Up the hill, obviously. She might still be about. She might be sitting on her doorstep eating ice-cream, and he would go up to her and say—

He shook his head. There was no situation, none, in which he could imagine himself speaking to her.

There was one. The crookedly printed notice in the cafe window was shouting at him, telling him so. Without taking time to think he plunged at the swing-door and was back inside the Gogo.

'Have you got anybody for evening work yet?'

Mr Antonio stared toffee-eyed at him through the steam of the coffee machine. 'No' yet,' he admitted at last.

'Can I have the job?'

There was a silence, as if all the old men and young couples were hanging on his every word. Mr Antonio said reasonably, 'We wis thinking of a lassie.'

'It doesn't say so in the notice,' said Eugene, very bold.

'Naw,' said Mr Antonio, giving him a long look. 'What you do, eh? You working?'

'I'm a clerk,' said Eugene.

'That no' enough work for you, eh?'

Eugene looked down at the floor and said, 'I'm saving up to get married.' The words came out quite without intention, and he knew as they left his lips that this was either the biggest lie or the deepest truth of his life.

'Okay,' said Mr Antonio suddenly. 'You start tomorrow, eh?'

Eugene nodded, then stopped in horror. His mother. How could he have forgotten, in God's name? 'The only thing is—' he said. 'I can't start till after the hospital visiting-hour.'

He waited in despair to hear that it was no use; but Mr Antonio only shrugged.

'That okay. Maria goes off at eight. You work eight to eleven, half-eleven, whenever we throw them out, right?'

'Right,' said Eugene, dazed with joy. He was half-way up the street when he remembered that he hadn't asked about wages. It didn't matter. Eight to eleven. Everybody came into the Gogo. She was bound to come in again. She would ask him for ice-cream and he would say—He stumbled upstairs to the empty house and threw himself on the bed. The dreams came galloping, green eyes, white skin, dark hair, honey voice and honey sweetness for no one but him. He flung his arms wide and let them come.

5

'It's too maddening,' said Helen, 'when you think that I'll have my licence in a couple of weeks.' Janet nodded: the formality of a driving test would not delay Helen long. They lay on the drawing-room floor with the plan of the city under their chins, all the great sprawl of houses and factories and churches and people tamed into black lines on white. 'But it's perfectly simple,' Helen said. 'I meet you in town and we get the number nineteen right down into Claggans.'

'Yes, I know,' said Janet. 'It's coming back at night I'm thinking about.'

'My goodness, Janet,' Helen said, 'it's light now till after eleven.'

'Even so,' Janet said. She very seldom argued with Helen: she always ended up hot, stupid, and of course defeated. 'We'll have to get different buses home. Mine is no use to you.'

Helen sighed so deeply that her trailing fair hair whisked the map like a fairy broom. 'That's what I'm showing you.' Her slim finger danced over the streets, still far too quickly for Janet to follow. 'Here's the church hall and here's the manse and *here's* your stop. You get the same bus back, the nineteen.'

'All right, but—'

'And *here* —The long fingernail, pale green today, traced a short neat curve. 'I walk through *here* for the number four. Look, it's no distance, about half an inch.'

'Yes, well, shouldn't take long to cover that,' said Janet.

Helen looked at her quite sharply and then dissolved into her sweet irresistible chuckle. 'You rascal, you made a funny,' she said. 'Well, okay, that's it, isn't it?' She got up from the floor in one movement; Janet heaved herself up rear first, irresistibly reminded of the conundrum about the cow. As she rubbed the indentation of the carpet out of her knees, Helen shot off down the corridor and was heard crying 'Mum, we're famished, how's food?'

'Ready when you are, sweetheart,' said her mother: she was always calm, but then, Janet thought, she would need to be. They all went into the dining-room and Helen's father, coming in from the study, flipped the dark and the fair heads with his folded newspaper as he passed.

'Well, girls, how's the command performance coming along?'

'Oh, great, Dad. We've got a two-hour programme worked out.' Helen propped her chin on her knuckles and talked bright-eyed on: her mother served soup, murmuring 'Janet, I know you'll take yours.' Janet was hungry, but she didn't like to start before Helen.

'—doing a guest turn. Yes, of course you know them, Paddy and *Ethne*, they were here at *Christmas*, that should pull in the crowds down there—'

'I hope,' said her father, 'the Reverend is prepared for an Irish immigration.'

'Well, we haven't quite told him yet, but he's so keen on co-operation and things, he won't mind.' Helen was starrily confident: never yet, Janet thought, had she met anybody who did mind. 'We're going to see him about it tomorrow night. Well, about fixing a date mostly.' She attacked her cooling soup, Janet following. 'At least,' she said through a spoonful, 'we hope we'll see him. The housekeeper person was a bit vague.'

'You could run them down there, couldn't you, darling?' said her mother, poking in a casserole with spoon and fork.

'Tomorrow?' Helen's father had one eye on his paper. 'Not tomorrow. It's the golf match over at Three Trees and I've to be there by six.'

'I thought that was Wednesday, darling.'

'No, Tuesday, I'm sure.' There was a hunt for a diary: 'Tuesday,' confirmed Helen's father, pleased. Like Helen, he was usually right.

'What a nuisance, darling.'

'Not at all,' said Helen, now ignoring her chicken casserole. 'It doesn't matter. I tell you it's not dark till half-past eleven. And we get the bus straight there and back. And there are two of us. And it's mid-week and there isn't a football match -'

Both her mother and her father were laughing by now. 'You know best, Helen,' her mother said.

'Yes,' said Helen, 'I do, don't I?'

'I sometimes think,' said her father to Janet, 'that we ought to have smacked her when she was three.' He looked sternly across the table at Helen, his pride and very joy.

Over the washing-up Janet said, 'Yes, but though we're going together—'

'Oh Janet, not again.'

'—we're coming back separately. You didn't tell your mum and dad that.'

'Really, Janet, I do assure you,' said Helen, splashing elbow-deep in far too much foam, 'you can't go telling them everything. They'd only worry, and that,' she said earnestly, 'wouldn't be fair, now would it?' She flicked suds at Janet's scowl. 'And it won't be dark till midnight, nearly,' she said.

In the sitting-room her father, leaning forward with a sigh to switch on his favourite programme, said, 'Where is it they're going, did you say?'

Her mother unrolled the Aran sweater she was knitting for Helen and slipped with moving lips into the weave of the pattern. 'A folk concert,' she said, 'in aid of something, you know, one of her things. In a church hall, but don't ask me where.'

'Sounds almost respectable for once,' said Helen's father.

'I expect she did tell me which one,' said Helen's mother. 'Yes, I'm sure she did.' She smiled at her knitting. 'Or else she thinks she did. You know Helen.' Blackberries grew under her needles, and the Tree of Life.

6

Kieron came slowly up the stair, the morning's paper rolled in his hand. Taking its first chance since the murder, it told you all that the Sundays had splashed, and a bit more. He had borrowed it from a mate at work and read it so hard and long that his friends had asked if he was doing the fashion competition. The boy who owned the paper had said 'For Christ's sake gie's the racing an' you can keep the rest,' and he had read it twice more on the bus coming home.

The door of their flat was standing ajar: as he paused, puzzled, Danny's tangled head appeared in the crack. When he saw Kieron he gave a loud sob. Tear-tracks shone on his dirty face and his nose was running. He hurled himself out of the house: he was nearly as tall as Kieron and his weight sent the two of them lurching against the stair-wall.

'What's up, son?' said Kieron in alarm. Danny sometimes got excited, but not as bad as this.

Danny gasped for words: he had been crying hard. 'It's my da—' he managed.

'Did he belt ye?'

'Naw—' Danny drove his fists into his eyes, a giant child. He gulped himself quiet. 'He's saying —I dinny ken what he's saying, Kieron.'

Kieron stood for a moment, rubbing the folded newspaper against his face. 'Well,' he said. 'We'd better see then.' There was no sound at all inside the house. 'You stay here, eh, Danny?'

But Danny, gasping and snuffling, would not stay behind. They went into the dark lobby together, where Danny had crouched smothering his sobs, waiting for Kieron's foot on the stair. The grey house was absolutely still. Kieron found that he was gripping the newspaper like a weapon, as if there was a mad dog behind the closed kitchen door. He pushed the door open and stood back.

Ah Christ, he thought as he did so, it's only my da.

Brady, sitting in the broken-springed armchair by the dead fire, looked up. He was dressed in shirt and trousers, and he was sober. 'Is it you, Kieron?' he said. 'What kept ye? I'm waiting for my tea.'

Nothing strange about him, no reason for Danny to stand staring at him in that frightened, unholy kind of awe. 'What did ye say to Danny?' Kieron said.

'Whit? Eh? Naethin',' said Brady, aggrieved. 'What's for the tea?'

Kieron, scowling uncertainly, looked from one to the other. 'Wait a minute,' he said. 'He was roaring an' greeting out in the lobby. Ye must have said something.'

'He was aye a big soft tumshie,' said Brady sulkily.

'For God's sake!' said Kieron. He discovered he was shouting. 'He was feart to come in! What did ye say?'

Brady snuffled and shrugged. 'Naethin',' he said. 'I was just telling him I seen your mammy.'

Kieron heard Danny behind him burst out in another noisy gulping sob. Anger at that surged up in him: he let it come, he whipped it up and urged it on. There was a black horror behind it, if it once slackened, that he could by no means face. 'Ye crazy old bugger, what are ye talking about?' he said.

'She looked great,' Brady said, musing. 'I wonder why she doesny come back.'

That finished Danny. He opened his mouth and howled helplessly, loud as a klaxon, abandoned to grief like a baby. Kieron turned on him and shouted 'Shut up!' and Danny with a shriek flung himself backwards into the lobby, to the open door. 'Mrs Sheehan!' he yelled.

She was already out on the landing. 'Kieron, son!' she said.

'It's no' me!' he said furiously. Fury was still the only safe thing. 'It's ma da, he's —I think he's —'

'All right, son,' she said. 'Take Danny in to my place. Bernie's there.'

Brady looked up eagerly: his face sagged into disappointed lines. 'Oh, it's you, Sarah,' he said. 'I thought it was Rose.'

Mrs Sheehan pushed Danny and Kieron out on to the landing and closed the door.

Bernie, wrapped neck to knee in an apron of her mother's was putting wee John into his dresser-drawer cot by the fire. Kieron stumbled in, pushing Danny in front of him: Danny was beside himself, weeping in great tearing spasms. Bernie without a word sat down in the big chair and held out her arms, and Danny fell on his knees beside her. She held him, rocking to and fro, pressing his face between her breasts as he cried.

Kieron stood with his back to the door. The anger and fear were hot in him: he could not take his eyes off Bernie and Danny. Her dark hair fell over her face and Danny's, comforting, sheltering. There had been plenty of girls before; but standing there across the kitchen from her, he felt Bernie Sheehan in every muscle and nerve.

Danny had cried himself out and was heaving with settling sobs. Kieron found himself listening for sounds from next door: nothing: what did he expect? A cramp gripped his left hand and he discovered that it was knotted in a fist. He began to rub his arm, slowly uncurling the stiff fingers. He was shaking and sore all over as if he had been kicked.

'That's better,' said Bernie gently, lifting Danny's heavy head to her shoulder. 'Sit up now. I'm going to make a cup of tea. You could do with one, couldn't you?' she said to Kieron. It was the first time she had looked at him: the warmth of her compassion, that had been all bent on Danny, flowed out to him and wrapped him in soft arms. Impossibly, they were still on opposite sides of the kitchen. 'I could do with something, Bernie,' he said, and hardly knew what he meant.

She took a meaning of a sort from it, and her cheeky smile flashed. 'Don't worry, I'll put a cinder in it,' she said. She slipped out of the chair and pulled Danny up to sit in it: he sat limply, his big hands hanging between his knees, occasionally raising an arm to draw a sleeve across his nose. His red eyes worshipfully followed Bernie's every move. Kieron, sitting down on the other side of the hearth, felt the stir of the old uneasiness.

Bernie poured the tea, lacing it with splashes of whisky. Kieron took the cup in both hands and drank deep. It tasted foul, but it stopped his shivering. He leaned his head against the back of the chair and listened again to the silence next door. He thought he heard the murmur of a voice, but it might have been only the groaning of the old building settling around them after the heat of the day. He thought, my God, there's another day like this tomorrow.

Wee John began to cry, and Bernie picked him up and held him to her, rocking gently, in much the same way as she had held Danny. She smiled over his silky head to Kieron, and he, a little light-headed from whisky and emotion, said 'My turn next?' Yesterday he might have said it cheekily to young Bernie in the park. Tonight, to this Bernie, he thought he meant it.

The door opened and closed, but Mrs Sheehan made no move to break the warm circle with Bernie at its heart. She poured herself a cup of tea, splashed in the whisky, and sat down heavily, her elbows on her knees.

'Do you really like that?' said Bernie to Danny. His face as he sipped the fortified tea was comically drawn.

'Do you?' said he.

'Come on an' we'll tip it down the sink,' said Bernie. 'Would you rather have some ice-cream?'

Danny nodded, smudging a left-over tear from his bright eye. Kieron looked at him and chewed his finger. Holy God, said the voice in his mind. Another six months and that goes out to work.

Bernie dumped the baby on her mother's lap. 'Danny an' me's going down to the Gogo,' she announced. 'Any of yez want a wafer?'

'Thanks,' said Mrs Sheehan, 'but we'll stick to the hard stuff,' and Bernie and Danny went off giggling like ten-year-olds. Their footsteps clattered down the two flights of stone stairs, and the silence of the crumbling tenement whispered back into the room.

'She's no' a bad lassie, Bernie,' said Mrs Sheehan eventually. She gave a half-laugh. 'But she's awfy like me.'

'I see that,' said Kieron. 'I see her like you.'

'Dae ye?' Mrs Sheehan glanced sideways at him. 'Aye, but I mean when I was her age.' She leaned forward in her chair, rolling the teacup between her hands, staring into the fire. 'Only she had it easier, some way. My faither beltit me stupid. An' Peter was labouring in the south, we had a hell o' a job getting hold of him in time. It was a toss-up would our first stop be the sacristy or the labour ward.' She laughed again, softly. 'So I canny be very cross about wee John.' She reached out for the whisky bottle and topped up their cups. 'God kens why I'm telling you this, Kieron. I doubt it's the whisky talking. But that's the way it is wi' Bernie an' me. A regiment couldny force us, but once we're started we wouldny hold back. No' a fingernail, no' a hair.'

'I see that too,' Kieron said. He sounded very tired. 'Mrs Sheehan,' he said, 'do ye ever wish ye could just go away?'

The embers in the grate crackled faintly and fell apart. Mrs Sheehan got up and leaned to put on more coal.

'If it's your da,' she said, 'I think he'll be all right now.'

'Does he ken—?'

'Oh, he kens now,' said Mrs Sheehan. 'I think he'll dae.'

'Then I'd better go over,' said Kieron. He got up and stood, hands on the mantelpiece, staring into the red heart of the fire. 'Mrs Sheehan, I shouldny have shouted at him. An' Danny — God, I nearly hit him. But I —I was awful worried.'

'I ken ye were, son.'

'It was that thing in the paper,' Kieron said. 'Did ye see it?'

'Aye,' said Mrs Sheehan. 'The Callaghan lassie. God be good to her.'

"It's the second in a month.'

'Aye, there's some beast going about,' said Mrs Sheehan. 'Please God they catch him soon.'

Kieron said, 'It was yesterday in the park put such a bloody scare in me. If he goes about doing that sort o' thing—' He bent his head still lower over the range. 'Mrs Sheehan,' he said. 'He goes out stravaiging at night. I canny keep him in. You wouldny — you wouldny think it was him ?'

'I wouldny,' said Mrs Sheehan. 'It wasny.' She stood up and her big hands rested lightly on Kieron's hunched shoulders, where the fine tremor had begun again. 'Put it out of your mind, son. Off you go home. He's a' right now.'

'Did ye manage to talk to him?' said Kieron.

Mrs Sheehan lifted the poker and touched up the slumbering fire, once, twice, with deft gentle thrusts. I didny do much talking,' she said. 'He wasny needing that.' The new coal murmured and fluttered into flame.

Kieron stumbled out on to the darkening landing and the pictures of the night blurred and dazzled before his eyes. Thin pretty Bernie and her fat mother, their concerned loving faces so different, so very alike. And Bernie comforting John, comforting Danny. And Mrs Sheehan comforting Brady: but that picture spun sparkling, unclear. And Bernie again, not even looking at him, away across the kitchen and near to him as his shivering skin. The pictures ran together in his tired mind, and were one picture after all.

Tuesday

Everyone was looking at them, Janet knew. What's this, eh, two birds on their own, not Gogo regulars either? But no one had lurched up to their table brandishing a flick-knife, no one had shouted insults, not a soul had tried to pick them up. They sat near the window and above the coffee-cups their bright eyes exchanged little excited messages. They were very brave, daring explorers, here in a cafe in the heart of the notorious Claggans. They hardly liked to admit that it might have been the ice-cream shop at the school gates.

Helen, handling her cigarette with expertise, said, 'Considering old useless wasn't there, we did get quite a lot done, didn't we?'

If he really had to go to a deathbed—' said Janet.

'Deathbed!' said Helen. 'He's forgotten all about us and gone to the pictures. Couldn't you tell by the look in the housekeeper's eye?'

'I'm sure you're wrong, Helen,' said Janet earnestly. 'Wouldn't he have taken the housekeeper with him?'

'Janet, you are a bundle of fun,' said Helen, 'are you in love or something?'

They snorted into their coffee-cups. Janet said 'No seriously —'

'Seriously—' mimicked Helen.

'The hall will do, won't it? Should take a couple of hundred —'

'Old useless will know, we'll ask him tomorrow—'

'Ought we to do something about tickets? They might turn up in droves—'

'Batter down the doors!' cried Helen in delight.

'Storm the stage—'

'We should be so lucky,' Helen said.

'No seriously, Helen, do you think we'll get many to come? Isn't it too hot to think of going to a concert?'

'Weeks to go yet, it may be snowing by then. Of course they'll come.'

'True enough it is for a good cause,' said Janet.

'It's a night out, more to the point,' Helen said. 'There can't be much left to do around here.'

'I suppose not,' said Janet dutifully. She really could not imagine how Helen would know that, two hours after stepping off the number nineteen bus.

'Well, they're flattening the place. Didn't you see as we walked down to the hall? We're just in time,' Helen said. For once you might almost have thought she was serious. 'In another couple of months there won't be anybody left.'

'I saw they'd pulled a lot of buildings down.' Janet was ashamed. She had walked quietly behind the housekeeper through the rubble and dust, seeing the boarded windows and the gappy tenements: seeing, not understanding. Helen, who had frisked alongside the woman and never for a moment stopped talking, had apparently seen something else. 'It's rather—' she said, and it was an effort for her, '—rather sad, in a way, isn't it?'

'Do you feel that too?' Helen said.

Janet said sensibly, "Of course they're going to new houses. Better houses. These are such terrible slums.'

'I know,' said Helen. They fell silent and looked round the crowded Gogo and out into the warm evening street. The Claggans, the dreaded Claggans, not frightening after all, not sinister, not violent, just dusty and hot and rather sad.

Helen got up for two more coffees. Strange how quickly you could get to know a place: here they were, already quite at home in the Gogo among the Claggans night people (because coffee after ten o'clock, to Janet and Helen, was the mark of a night person). Not drunks, not hooligans, not monsters, said Janet's and Helen's secret looks to one another. Some were a little odd-looking, like the fat sweating woman billowing over a tiny table towards a very pregnant girl. Some were dirty, like the old tramp in the corner soaking biscuits in his tea; but Helen and Janet had been educated to pity rather than blame. Some were perfectly normal, like the fair-haired young man reading a detective story over his egg and chips. Janet's eyes went back to him as he thoughtfully forked up chips and drank tea, quite absorbed in his book. He looked serious, he looked studious. She wondered if he might be a little lonely.

The oddest of the lot, really, was the man behind the counter, his pale face gleaming with sweat under his very black hair as he wrestled unskilfully with the coffee machine. He didn't appear to be entirely at home in his job. He looked up every time the door opened.

Silly to expect, Eugene kept telling himself, that she'd be in every night. But some night, some night she was bound to come in. Why, she'd said so herself. In this hot weather you bought lemonade and ice-cream, in all weathers you bought fish suppers and crisps, and if you lived in the Claggans it was in the Gogo that you bought them. Stand long enough behind this steamy counter and you'd see everyone in the Claggans. Half the faces here Eugene knew from the public library. The others were, by their look, Gogo regulars: except perhaps the two girls by the window, who had given themselves away by sitting down first instead of ordering at the counter. His heart had jumped when he saw the dark head in the doorway, but this was a fat girl, round-faced and plain, sitting mooning around the cafe while her little blonde friend chattered on. He was certainly seeing more girls in this job than ever before. Time was when they were so scarce in his life that even sitting beside one on a bus was enough to start him off. Funny how it meant nothing to him now: there was only the one girl for him. That was how you recognized the real thing, of course.

He looked up, but it was only a small boy wanting a sixpenny cone. What if she came in every night before he started work at eight o'clock? Ah, but everything had fallen in so well up to now: God wouldn't let that happen, Eugene thought.

Brady mumbled his softened biscuits and drew in great sups of tea. You would think a man could go home and sit by his own fireside of an evening, not sicken hisself with Gogo dishwater. But no fears, not with Lord Muck playing at God Almighty. Tonight he had said—what was it again?

Brady snuffled indignantly at his tea. What Kieron had said escaped him now, but it had been a bloody insult anyway, and Brady had said so of course. And then Kieron had said — of this

Brady was sure enough — 'I didny mean nothing, ye touchy old sod.' Now was that a way to speak to your faither? Be damned was it! That young bastard needed sorting out, so he did. Ah God, for the strength to dae it. Brady wept a few tears into the Gogo tea.

Mary Lynch said, all excited, 'I'm awful pleased for you, Mrs Sheehan. A beginner's aye lucky. I wis sure you'd have a win.'

'It's a shame though, so it is,' said Mrs Sheehan, laughing. 'You that comes every second night, an' it's me that gets the win.' Ten pounds, she thought, it'll no' put a roof on the cottage, but it's something.

'Ach, get away, there's aye the next night. Did ye like it, though?' said Mary. Her thin face was quite pink and she was as giggly as if she had won herself. The fellow behind the counter had looked apprehensive as her great bulk lumbered through the door, and Mrs Sheehan could hardly blame him. The fifth wee Lynch seemed likely to appear on the Gogo floor at any moment.

'Oh aye, I liked it fine, Mary,' she said.

'You'll come again, eh?'

Mrs Sheehan said in spite of herself, 'How long will you be carrying on?'

'Ah, another three weeks I'm sure,' said Mary with a gay laugh. 'I'm cheating that way, it's the muscles being slack. I'm no' as far along as you'd think.'

'Just as long as ye feel up to it, Mary.'

'I wouldny miss it,' said Mary. If you looked at her from the shoulders up, she was thin and eager and touching as a schoolgirl; God, she was little more. But Mrs Sheehan was not so sure about the bingo. It was a night out, right enough; there was the chance, paraded constantly before you, of winning the snowball: all she needed, practically, ready to fall into her lap. Only she had looked round the queue as they waited outside the bingo hall; young, middle-aged, old women, pressing forward, eager-faced. What was it she had seen in those faces? They were only Claggans women, her neighbours; but 'I don't know, Mary,' she said. 'I wonder could I ever get to be as keen as those folk.'

Mary's narrow mouth drooped a little. 'It passes the time great,' she said.

And Mrs Sheehan saw her again with the dirty, wailing babies round her feet, and that coarse lump Eddie Lynch drunk in the background. God, of course the lassie liked her bingo. 'Oh, sure I'll come with ye again, Mary,' she said. 'Only tell me if ye see me getting one o' thae bingo faces.'

'Eh?' said Mary, smiling, ready to see the joke.

Quinn sat with his book open beside his plate, but he was not reading. Nothing new in that. Now and again he drew out a diary and made a note, like the notes he sometimes scribbled in his order book in the library. He often smiled to think how surprised they'd be to see those scribbles, the prim library girls. And that particular library girl, the blonde who'd got him going, would be surprised at his thoughts now.

God, she was easy to play. He could strum her like a guitar. He had only to drop his voice a tone or two, and the great fringy eyelashes were at it again. A sheltered only child was Lisa (he had got her name with no trouble), dying to come out of the shelter and start living. One push and she'd be over. Not so much as a push.

So, though for the second successive day they had had quite a chat at eleven o'clock and again at four, he hadn't made a date with her yet. She might be wondering why, because she had worked hard enough for it: but no, perhaps she was too dumb to know what she'd asked for. Tomorrow, in any case, she would have her reward. She was panting for it, for God's sake. No point wasting time, thought Quinn, turning a page of his detective story.

'Look at the time!' Janet cried. The sad Claggans street was still shining with long summer twilight, but it was already half-past ten. 'We'll have to go, Helen, my mother — your mother —'

'But they know where we are.'

'That's just the trouble,' Janet said.

They stood at Janet's bus-stop in the warm dusty evening. 'Go and get your own bus,' Janet said. 'This is keeping you awfully late.'

'Not a bit of it,' said Helen. 'Same bus tomorrow and hope old useless is in this time?'

The housekeeper *promised*,' Janet said. 'And we'll have coffee again to celebrate, because it's my turn to pay.'

Helen, following the map in her head, walked away from the bus-stop and turned right. Streets that had been black lines on paper unrolled around her: there was the one she wanted, the dog-leg of high grey tenements, quiet but lined with street-lamps; nothing to worry about there. Again she felt like a daring explorer, and her chart was not wrong. She hitched up her shoulder-bag and stepped out with more than her usual swagger; oh Helen, so you're a little nervous after all, are you? she thought.

She looked about with bright interested eyes and, as she knew it would, the nervousness went. See, the houses at this end still have people in them: wonder how it feels, sitting there watching the demolishers come. See, there's a bingo hall, closed now of course. They'll be glad to come to our concert instead. And it's for a good cause; they're very generous down here. There you go again, Helen, 'they', as if they were a different species. And poor Janet always being scolded for that.

Her short summer skirt flirted round the corner of the street: no distance now. An alley ran off to the left, and at its far end she could actually see the shop-windows and buses of the main road. Cut down there to save time? But she was already past the opening, so quickly she was walking: not worth going all the way back. Oh well, remember it for tomorrow. Empty houses, a wilderness of waste ground here on either side: then a church, then houses with curtains at their windows again, and there was the main road.

A number four bus, the kind with an open platform too, had stopped at the lights. She ran and jumped, all arms and legs, and laughed up at the conductor, who looked as if he might have been thinking of putting her off. He laughed too and said 'Okay, sweetheart,' and people looked round smiling, and the bus sailed on in triumph, the explorer going home.

'So you see it was perfectly all right,' she said to her mother. 'Only we'll have to go back tomorrow, because old useless wasn't in. But everyone was so sweet to us, in the cafe, everywhere —'

'Was that the minister you were talking about?' her father said, looking over his glasses.

'And all those empty houses, and people being moved out,' Helen said. 'Even Janet thought it was quite sad.' She gave a little giggle, and then stuffed her handkerchief into her mouth. Because she felt a little guilty, always laughing at Janet.

Wednesday

1

The girl Lisa and the fair-haired young salesman were talking to each other at the counter; quietly of course, because they were in the reading-room after all, but talking none the less. That being so, she could hardly check other folk for doing the same. Could she? Mad Mac leaned across the table, a hand shielding his eager mouth, and told old Moses and Pat Brady a long and very dirty joke.

'Think shame, ye ruttin' old goat,' said Moses mildly.

'Ach well,' said Mac, peering at the counter over his string-mended glasses. 'I bet he's telling her a worse yin.'

'I wouldny be surprised,' said Moses. 'I'm no' very keen on that lad.'

'You're just jealous!' crowed Mad Mac. The idea appealed to him tremendously and he began to laugh and cough together, muffling his splutters in the torn lining of his cap.

'I'm telling ye,' said Moses, 'ye're sex-daft. Is he no', Pat?'

Brady said dully 'Eh? I dunno,' and relapsed into his hunched, gloomy, staring silence. Moses looked at him for a moment. Pat had always been a bit funny —the war hadny helped — and more so since he came back and found his wife the way she was. But this was different. He had maybe been batting about before like a clockwork toy set off in the wrong direction; but now you would say someone had taken out the spring.

Moses hawked delicately and, since Lisa was not looking, spat into the corner behind the table. 'Are you okay thae days, Pat?' he said.

'Mind your own bloody business,' said Brady.

He said it very loudly, almost shouting, and it was obviously more than Lisa could overlook. 'Would you keep quiet please!' she called across the room. The young man made no move at all, looking neither at the old men nor at his girl-friend, but staring out of the dusty window with a bored expression on his handsome face. That's a cold bastard, old Moses thought. Pity help the lassie if she thinks she's got him.

The man and the girl turned back to their talk and Mad Mac said 'Bitch' under his breath. Pat Brady gloomed at him, but it was hard to tell if the gloom was any deeper than usual. It was mid-morning; the old men were the only readers in the high square room, not yet directly sunlit. Above the heavy dark counter the man's gold head and the girl's fair one shone in their own young light.

Old Moses said defiantly and quite loudly, 'He minds me o' somebody, but I canny think who.'

Lisa sighed and lifted her head. She said firmly, 'I'm afraid you'll really have to go out.' She stared straight at the three old men.

Moses saw that her prim mouth was trying hard not to tremble. Buggered if the lassie wasny scared stiff: and a lot of help her fancy boy was, standing there like Nelson's bloody column. 'That's okay,miss,' he said, and nudged the other two towards the door. He might have said more: but a kindness had crept into his voice already, and he didn't think she liked that much.

2

Quinn, coming in, had stopped for a moment inside the door of the reading-room, looked round for an empty table (though there were plenty this morning), cat-neat and handsome, with his brief-case under his arm. Lisa saw him at once, but she bent her head over her work. He never came first to speak to her, and she certainly wasn't going to lie down in his path. You mustn't appear too eager, anybody knew that.

Still she could not quite help the blush, the wicked deep little flutter, when she saw that gold head in the doorway. Miss Grierson frowned on holding hands across the counter, and anyway Lisa considered herself past that stage; but Quinn, ah, Quinn was different. Older, for one thing, than the boys she had gone out with before. Far more sophisticated, more self-possessed. When he stood at the counter and looked at you with those clear blue eyes, you really didn't know what he was thinking.

But he must be thinking something. Wednesday today: for two

days now, whenever she was on reading-room duty, sooner or later he had appeared at the door; sooner or later he had come over to the counter. He had his routine; she thought that order and routine must mean a lot to him, so neat he was, so self-contained. He would look over the room, sit down at a distant table, spread out his books, work for a bit; she sometimes wondered what exactly he could be writing, with such intent effort that his face flushed and his blue eyes stared. Then she would look up to find that he had crossed the room silently and was standing above her with his clear waiting gaze. Oh, he was thinking of something, that was sure.

Yet he hadn't said much so far. Perhaps it wasn't his way to be very talkative. (He was only Quinn still, for instance: if he had another name, he wasn't telling.) He stood and let her talk, and listened to her, and nodded his handsome head, and now and again almost smiled. Well, twice a day, and this was the third day; he must like her a little, Lisa thought. Deep down she felt the flutter again, the butterflies, the thrill. Perhaps something was really going to come of it. Perhaps this was the real thing.

And he had done it again. He was standing at the desk, his brief-case poised under his fingers, looking steadily at her with light, bright, disturbing eyes. 'Hello, Quinn,' she said, smiling up at him. 'How are you today?'

'Very well, thank you,' said Quinn. He had this odd trick of never asking how you were in return. He stood there, not speaking; still, he must be happy enough, or he wouldn't stay. Lisa kept the conversation going in a suitably muted reading-room tone, and he nodded and looked quite interested, and even asked a few questions. 'Do you live far from here?' he asked, and 'Do you have much late work in this job?' Both good questions, Lisa felt; surely pointing only one way? And at last he asked, apropos of nothing in particular, 'What do you do with yourself in the evenings, Lisa?'

That was the moment one of the dirty old men muttering at the other end of the room had to choose to begin shouting and swearing. Lisa winced and called 'Would you keep quiet please!' He subsided, grumbling, and she looked sideways at Quinn. This was a beastly job sometimes: she hoped she hadn't sounded too bitchy. But Quinn, taking no notice, was staring absently out of the window.

Now, Lisa, careful. Not too eager, remember. Be sophisticated, be self-possessed, do the proper thing. 'Sorry, Quinn,' she said, 'what were you saying?' He did not reply.

She could have killed that old man. But surely she didn't have to leave it there? Only polite, after all, to answer Quinn's question. 'Oh,' she said, exactly as if he had responded, 'about what I do in the evenings? The usual, I suppose. This time of year it's nice to get out into the park.' He still said nothing, and she said with a touch of desperation, 'Though the cinemas are air-conditioned, it's quite nice there too.' He smiled and made as if to speak; and another of those *bloody* old men had to open his big mouth.

I'm afraid,' said Lisa furiously, 'you'll really have to go out.'

They went very quietly after all: the tall old Jew with the long black greasy hair shepherded his companions out, though not without some parting crack or other. She didn't think she had been too much of the martinet librarian. She turned back to Quinn, parting her lips. His strong smooth fingers drummed on the brief-case handle.

At last he said, 'Working late tonight, Lisa?'

'No, not tonight,' she said, 'Friday this week.'

'Good. Would you meet me after work tonight then?'

Her heart gave one big thump, quite surprising her. She hadn't been wrong. But Lisa, take it easy. He mustn't get the idea you were waiting for it.

'Oh Quinn,' she said, prettily regretful, 'not *tonight*. I'm sorry I just can't make it. But . . .'

She let her voice trail off invitingly. That's it, Lisa, honour is satisfied, and no flustering about hair-washing or phone calls. Now he had only to say 'Well, what about tomorrow? ...or Friday?...or . . .'

But he didn't. He stood still and looked at her with those light eyes. She had the queerest feeling that he had stopped seeing her. A dark-red flush rose in his face. She could not quite believe it: she had never seen a person nearer going purple with rage. His eyes grew wider. If he had not been such a good-looking young man, she would almost have said that they were bulging. Without another word, he turned and walked out of the library.

Lisa was astounded. After all her care to do the proper thing! You couldn't accept a date for this very night, now could you ? 'Really!' she said crossly after him. 'You don't need to take it like that.'

3

Wee Pauline was girny. She stumped around the pale-blue dream kitchen, and scraped the side of her foot along the vinyl floor-tiles, and kicked the table leg, and moaned 'Mammy, can I get out to play?'

'No, you can not,' said Annie abstractedly. She slapped the haddock fillets from egg to breadcrumbs and turned down the heat under the pan. Her mind was on none of these things. For the twelfth time she made to pick up the letter from the kitchen cabinet, and remembered once again just in time to draw back her eggy hands.

'How no', Mammy?'

'How no' what?'

'How can I no' get out to play?'

'Your tea's ready, that's how no'.'

'It is nutt ready.'

'It'll be ready when your daddy comes in.'

'You said it was ready now,' howled Pauline. 'You telt a lie. You'll go to hell.'

'You'll go straight to your bed–'

What with the slap and the roaring, neither of them heard the lift. 'Well, lassies,' said James, 'what's up then?' and they fell back sniffing and sobbing. He laughed – but nobody ever took offence at James's laugh – at the two round fair miserable faces, so ridiculously alike.

Annie broke away to attend to the frying-pan, shaking it with cross little jerks. 'She's been a right wee pest since she came home,' she said, gulping.

'Pauline,' said James, 'that's terrible.' He kissed Annie on the ear and sat down; Pauline climbed hiccupping on to his knee. 'Just let me get my tie off. That's better. My word, this heat, it's no' good for you.'

'Very hot the day,' said Annie, turning the fish in the pan.

'So it is.'

'Hot yesterday an' a'.'

'Aye,' said James, looking at her carefully.

'I wonder will it be hot–'

'So what's up then, lass?' said James.

'Nothing,' said Annie, sobbing above the frying fish.

James put the small girl off his knee with a pat on the behind. 'Pauline,' he said, 'away and look in my jacket, you'll maybe find a sweetie.' He crossed the floor and put his hands on Annie's cushiony hips. 'Okay, hen, tell us.'

Annie said, waning, 'I had a letter from my mammy.'

'A *letter*?'

'Why not?' said Annie. She was prickly, but it had dried her eyes at least.

'Just,' said the peaceable James, 'that we saw her on Saturday and it's only Wednesday now.' He paused and his stroking hands moved to her shoulders. 'Nothing wrong, is there?'

'No. Aye. Ach, read it yourself,' said Annie. She wiped her hands on her apron, dabbed a knuckle under her eyes, and took the letter from under the biscuit-tin. She turned away and made a great business of serving the fish, while James, in puzzlement, read.

'Dear Annie just to let you know,' Mrs Sheehan had written, 'that Bernie has come back and she has a baby, its daddy is a seafaring man. Her and John is going to stay for a while. We are hoping for to get a wee house in the country as soon as we have the money, we will let you know, your loving mother Sarah Sheehan. PS. John is the baby.'

'Well?' demanded Annie.

'Well what?' said James cautiously.

'You know what I mean!' cried Annie. Pauline, her cheek distorted round a sweetie, came big-eyed back into the kitchen. Annie lowered her voice. 'What wee house? What money? What's she *talking* about, James?'

James, upturning the tomato sauce bottle over his plate, stopped and said 'My God.' A huge gout of sauce slid out of the bottle and swamped the fish. Pauline giggled wildly. Annie, distracted, tutted and frowned at them both.

"She was on about that on Saturday,' James said. 'Talking about a country cottage. Something I said started her off. Something about retiring to a but an' ben.'

'But getting the money!' said Annie in despair. 'She hasny a ha'penny. How much does she think it would cost, a wee house like that?'

'She thinks,' said James shamefaced, 'it would cost five hundred pounds.'

Annie put her fists on her hips and looked down at him. 'Something else you said?'

'I never said five hundred—' said James. His honest face was worried; he sat poking at his fried fish and searching his conscience. 'Well, I did. But I never meant —First figure that came into my head. I never imagined—'

'Well, she hasny got it anyway,' said Annie wearily, sitting down to the ruins of her tea, 'and I canny see her getting it, unless in the Irish Sweep. It must be just a notion she's got hold o'. It'll pass.'

James's brow cleared. 'You're right,' he said, 'of course. What am I worrying about? Five hundred pounds! She's as likely to get five thousand.'

He turned to his tea with a fresh appetite. It was Annie who sat glooming now, pushing the fish about her plate, never noticing how Pauline left half of hers and went straight on to the iced cakes.

'James,' she said at last. 'Can you get cottages nowadays very easy?'

'Funny enough the boys were only talking about that the other day,' said James cheerfully. 'Likely what put it into my head. A' the toffs are buying up cottages now. You canny get one for love nor money.'

'No' for five hundred pounds?'

'Wouldny look near it,' James said, spreading strawberry jam on his bread.

4

They heard the whistling first, a gaily syncopated version of 'Faith of Our Fathers', and then the hop, skip and jump on the stairs. Danny, giving wee John his bottle, looked up and said joyfully, 'That's Kieron coming in.'

'Give him a shout, Bernie,' said Mrs Sheehan, 'or he'll wonder where Danny is.'

'You don't suppose he'll guess?' said Bernie.

Kieron from the door called 'Are ye there, Danny?' He came bouncing in, uncommonly tousled and cheerful: Bernie dodged, but did not quite avoid a comradely slap and cuddle. 'Where's ould Paddy?' he said, bright-eyed.

'Out,' said Danny.

'Ah well, we'll chip him in,' said Kieron. He dragged from his pocket a fistful of pound notes, peeled off two and pushed them into Danny's hand. 'Away down to the Gogo an' get us five chicken suppers an' some lemonade.'

'Kieron,' said Danny, staring aghast at the notes. 'It's only Wednesday.'

Mrs Sheehan chuckled and said, 'We used to call it the day before tomorrow, only it was Thursday then.'

'I know,' said Kieron. He stretched his arms luxuriously above his head, riffling the money in his hand. 'I got a great tip today. Rags to Riches at thirty-three to one. Waltzed it. The rest's still running.'

'Did ye, Kieron?' said Mrs Sheehan. 'Here, sit down, son, an' tell us a' about it.'

'Ye've to watch my mammy,' said Bernie, taking wee John from Danny and putting him over her shoulder. 'Don't you know she's a hard gambler thae days?'

'Ah, Kieron,' protested Mrs Sheehan. 'I was at the bingo last night. To hear her ye'd think it was strip poker.'

'Had ye any luck?'

'Just ten pounds.'

'Just!' said Kieron. 'What do ye usually get, the snowball?'

Mrs Sheehan giggled like a girl. 'Ah, Kieron, it was my first time. I was hoping for tae win five hundred pounds.'

'Oh ye were, were ye?' said Kieron. 'Ye'd have given the rest back?'

'Five hundred's a' I want,' said Mrs Sheehan. 'Ye see —' He

wasn't going to laugh at her, was he? 'When we get that,' she said, 'Bernie an' me, we're buying a country cottage.'

'Allow you!' said Kieron, raising his eyebrows. 'Is that what they cost, then?'

'Annie's James says so. Ye see—' She began again, about the garden and no stairs, the fireside with the rag rug, the primroses in the brass kettle. Bernie gave a bit of a laugh — well, she had heard it a few times by now —and moved away to change wee John. Kieron leaned forward in his chair, lively and interested and very slightly drunk, and listened without laughing at all.

'Well, you're a topper, Mrs Sheehan,' he said. 'When is it ye're flitting?'

'I've got to get the five hundred pounds first.'

'Another forty-nine goes at the bingo an' you're home.'

'Och, Kieron, ye're kidding,' said Mrs Sheehan. 'Listen, though.' She stopped and looked sideways at him: no, he wasn't laughing. 'If ye a' think I'm a gambler,' she said, 'I might as well carry on. Only I'm no' accustomed to bookies an' that. If I give ye some money will you put it on for me?'

'Are ye serious? Aye,' said Kieron, 'I can see ye are.' He looked at her thoughtfully, a little sobered. 'The only thing is,' he said, 'you'll maybe have heard, they dinny always win.'

'I'll pick a good yin,' said Mrs Sheehan, beaming.

'My God,' said Kieron, 'we'll see you yet wi' your bunnet on back to front. Okay, look. There's a big race on tomorrow. They're bound to be on about it in the day's paper.'

'I'll pick ma fancy then.'

'You do that,' said Kieron. 'We'll get the morra's paper first thing for the card an' the prices, an' I'll see this fella at work.'

'Will I give you the money now, Kieron?'

'No,' said Kieron. 'God forgive me, but I wouldny risk half-a-dollar o' yours in the house wi' —' He caught Danny's innocent gaze. 'Wi' the mice,' he said, 'they'd have it chewed down to a tanner.' Danny giggled.

'I'll give ye a knock then,' said Mrs Sheehan. 'I'm aye about early.'

'Okay,' said Kieron. He reached out a toe and poked Danny.

'How about those chicken suppers, eh, Mac?'

'I'll go down with him,' said Bernie, tucking wee John into his drawer. 'He'll never carry five on his own.'

'I'll come too,' said Kieron, jumping up. Bernie slid him her green glance and said 'Ah, okay.'

They walked side by side down the long street: Danny skipped and jumped like a happy elephant. Kieron, scliffing stones ahead of him with the edge of his foot, chuckled to himself.

'What are you giggling at?' enquired Bernie.

'Oh, your mammy,' said Kieron, 'an' her five hundred pound.'

'Don't you dare laugh at my mammy!' cried Bernie.

'Aw, God, Bernie,' said Kieron, stopping in dismay, 'I'm no' laughing that way. I wouldny laugh at your mammy. She's the greatest.'

'That's okay then,' said Bernie in a light little half-offended voice. They walked on silently. Kieron had stopped scliffing his stones.

He said after a few minutes, 'But —'

'But what?'

'Don't get me wrong, Bernie. But does she really mean it?'

'Oh aye,' said Bernie, 'far as I can see,' and she permitted herself a little chuckle this time.

'An' you'd go with her?'

'I'd need to, wouldn't I?'

Kieron found a fist-sized stone in his path and kicked it so that it rattled from lamp-post to wall and back. 'A country cottage, eh,' he said, 'I hope it's no' beyond a bus-route.'

'Why?' said Bernie suspiciously.

'Well, I'd need to buy a bike,' said Kieron. After a moment Bernie said, 'Cheeky big brother you've got, Danny.'

'I would need to buy a bike too, Bernie.'

'Ah,' said Bernie, 'you're a hell of a pair.' She sounded absolutely delighted. 'Well, watch it then. Else we'll move to an island, an' you'll have to buy a boat.'

They walked on pleasantly enough; but at the Gogo door Bernie cried, 'Right, Danny, in we go.'

'I half thought I was coming in too,' said Kieron mildly. 'Oh please yourself,' said Bernie. 'Danny an' me will manage, but you could hold the door.'

Well, ye wee besom, Kieron thought. He stood scowling at the door as Bernie's clear high voice gave the order. She was even, hell mend her, batting her eyelashes at the fella behind the counter, who was behaving very oddly. He didn't seem able to take his eyes off Bernie. He made three tries at scooping the last chicken portion out of the hot fat.

Danny said, 'I think I've lost the money.'

'Okay,' said Kieron. 'I'll wait outside, will I, while you sort that out?' He knew he was not being at all fair to Danny.

After a few moments of flurry, the two pound notes were found in Danny's hip pocket. The man at the counter gave him a handful of silver in change: Bernie, inquisitive as ever, said, 'Hey, that should be another bob, surely?'

Kieron, glooming from the door, felt almost sorry for the man: covered in confusion was a mild way to put it. He took the change back, raked about in the till, counted it into his own hand, recounted it into Danny's, got it wrong again, and finally, with audible assistance from Bernie, came to some solution.

'I'm awful sorry, miss,' he said in a crushed voice.

'That's all right,' said Bernie, 'it's easy done,' and, fluttering her eyelashes again, she gave the miserable man a full-scale come-hither smile. Ah, damn her anyway, Kieron said to himself.

The light was on in the Bradys' house when they got back. Kieron hesitated on the landing.

'I'd better go in with his chicken supper,' he said. 'He's that bloody touchy thae days, ye wouldny know how to take him.'

'Bring him in, Kieron,' called Mrs Sheehan from the kitchen.

'Are ye sure, Mrs Sheehan?'

'I've telt ye afore,' she said.

Brady was sitting at the kitchen table, his chin nearly on the oilcloth, champing at a doorstep of bread and margarine. A handleless cup of black tea stood at his elbow. He glanced up, when Kieron came in, with bleary old eyes.

'Mrs Sheehan says are ye coming in, Da?' Kieron said. 'There's a chicken supper for ye.'

Brady did not seem to have heard. 'Whit the hell's the use o' having sons?' he demanded. 'Wad it hurt ye to be here when I come in once in a bloody while?'

'I would be, Da,' said Kieron, 'if I'd any idea when ye'd be coming.'

'Oh aye', said Brady. 'Never heed. I ken you're too busy hooring next door.'

Kieron said after a moment, 'Do you want your chicken supper?'

'Stuff yer chicken supper,' said Brady. He got up, swept the cup and plate off the table with a jerk of his coat-sleeve, and limped out of the room. Kieron stood gripping the back of a chair, listening as the uneven footsteps hurried downstairs.

'He's away out again,' he said to Mrs Sheehan's worried look.

'I suppose,' she said, 'he didny say where.'

Kieron said, 'Buggered if I care.'

Much as Mrs Sheehan tried to keep the party going, they ate the chicken suppers in low spirits. Kieron only nibbled at his: finally he pushed the cardboard plate over to Danny.

'Eat the rest, son. An' get yourself to bed when Mrs Sheehan chucks ye out, will ye?'

'Where are ye going?'

'Nae idea,' said Kieron.

'Kieron,' said Mrs Sheehan.

'Aye?' said Kieron at the door.

'Ye'll mind ye've to back that horse for me the morra?'

Kieron laughed. 'I wasny intending to get wheeled hame on a barra,' he said. 'I'm just taking a walk around.' He looked over at Danny, blissfully finishing his second chicken supper. 'If I knock across the old fella, I suppose I'll see what he's up tae,' he said.

5

Eugene wiped the counter top and thought about her; as if he ever thought about anything else now. They were brother and sister, he told himself for the millionth time, she and the boy. Both so dark, and she so offhand with him. And the young boy was brother to both of them. There it was, the family. Stood to reason.

No need to worry about that.

He looked up at his next customer, straight into the dark face of the boy who had been with Bernie.

'Coffee.'

'Coffee, sir,' said Eugene. He fumbled with the handles of the coffee machine. Take it easy now, no need to appear a holy idiot altogether. The fella would go back and tell his sister, that's a right odd sod behind the Gogo counter. And she would laugh — No, she wouldn't. You could tell from her face she was kind and good. Eugene passed over the coffee, slopping half of it into the saucer.

The boy did not seem to notice either that or Eugene's frantic efforts to dry and replace. 'Tell me, Mac,' he said, absently counting out the money, 'did ye see an old man in here the night?'

'What kind of an old man?'

The boy hesitated. 'He'd be wearing a grey coat down to his feet nearly. A bunnet. A muffler.' He paused again. 'No' very clean looking,' he said, rather low.

Eugene looked suspiciously at him. Where did a dirty old man fit into the happy family circle?

'An old fella with a limp? Drank his tea out the saucer?'

'Aye,' said the boy with a sigh, 'that's him.'

'Oh aye, he was in a while ago.' Eugene drew his brows down, contemplating the young man and his odd questions. It would be a pity if Bernie's brother was mixed up in anything, well, shady. Another thought struck him, and, inspired by dim memories of bar-tenders in old films, he said, 'Hey, you're no' the cops, are ye?'

'Holy God,' said the young man. 'What was he doing?'

'Nothing,' said Eugene hastily. 'He was in earlier on. Didny stay long. Been gone half an hour.'

'Ah to hell,' said the young man, 'I'll never find him now,' and he slumped with his coffee into a chair facing the wall. Even his back view looked weary: he freed one foot from its dusty shoe and worked it up and down. Eugene saw a hole in his sock, rubbed over a blistered heel. If he was looking for that dirty old tramp - though why he should be was a mystery to Eugene - he had walked himself nearly into the ground.

And over in the far corner sat another gloomy young man: one of the regulars, as Eugene had already begun to call them. Tonight was no night, apparently, for egg and chips and a nice library book. The fair young man had ordered a pot of coffee, and he was not reading but thinking, joined fingers pressed against his lips as he sat with his elbows on the table. He was not even drinking his coffee. Occasionally his lips moved in a silent word or two.

Oddly enough his shoes were dusty too, and the trouser-legs white with dust for three inches above the cuffs, as if he too had done a good bit of walking tonight in the dry dirty Claggans streets. Eugene had a queer picture of the Claggans, this hot summer night, laid out like a chess-board, with dirty old men and morose young men doggedly making their moves, up, down and across. Perhaps this one was in love. Eugene sent him a thought of sympathy. How good it was, after all the lonely years, to feel, just like anyone else, the sweet pangs of love!

The blond young man was staring absently at the table by the window. The two girls were there again, the little fair one fizzing with chat, even her fat friend quite worked up for once. But they weren't Claggans girls, Eugene was sure, if only because of their high confident polite voices. It wasn't likely the young man knew them. He seemed to be looking very steadily at them, but it must be only chance.

Helen and Janet were the happiest people in the Gogo. Helen was saying 'Two shows! We'll rake it in, old Janet, we can't turn down an offer like that.' And Janet in the midst of her rejoicing had suddenly got stage-fright. 'That's four hundred people!' she kept saying. 'It's too many, we can't do it.' She clasped her plump arms over her head and groaned. 'Helen, it's getting out of hand.'

'Last night you were worried in case nobody would come.'

'Well, perhaps they won't.' Janet veered, giggling hysterically, between the two awful possibilities. 'You said everyone's moved out of the Claggans. There won't be four hundred people left.'

'That's where the publicity comes in. You heard him say it could be announced from every pulpit on the South Side. Janet, what a thing, eh?' Helen clapped her hands, laughing: even the solemn man behind the counter had to twitch a smile. 'I never have seen myself starting university in October, you know that? Let's go into show-business instead.'

Janet ignored this: sometimes, with Helen, you just had to. 'I wonder if they'll let us put up a poster in the café here?'

'Of course they will. I know,' said Helen, 'once we get the posters printed we'll come down with an armful and go round all the shops.'

'Now we know our way about,' said Janet. They nodded at each other in grave delight: the terrible Claggans, a paper tiger after all. Helen stretched happily and said, "Getting late—' but they had no urge to move. They sat over their coffee-cups, looking out of the cafe window, observing still as the Claggans evening drew into night.

For it was late enough. Eugene glanced at his watch under cover of a dish-towel. It was after eleven: he seldom got home now before midnight. 'Looking tired, son,' his mother had croaked at visiting-time, and he had said, 'It's missing you, Mammy.' Whether that was a white one or matter for confession he had not yet decided. There was so much more to think about nowadays.

It was late enough, anyway, for the girls. They got up, arguing little as girls always did, and went out, laughing still, full of their own affairs. The blond young man finally drank off his cold coffee and left too. Except for the hell-raising teenagers in the back, there was no one left in the Gogo but Eugene, and Bernie's brother.

For he must be Bernie's brother. Eugene weighed him up, measured him, tried to fit Bernie's delicate features into the frame of his broader masculine bones. Yes, brother and sister they must be. Mustn't they?

The boy got up to go. Now was the chance: one question, half-a-dozen words, would settle it, Eugene knew. But he could not ask it. He might get the wrong answer, and then what would he do?

6

The number nineteen bus veered and bore towards them under full sail, and Janet said all in a rush, 'Come on this one with me.'

'Janet, my poppet, what are you thinking about? It's no use to me, this one.'

'You can change in town. Come on, Helen. It's too late for you to go home from here alone.'

'They didn't get me last night, did they?' And as Janet teetered with one foot in the gutter, 'Look he's starting. Are you going to run behind all the way to the Square?'

With a heave and a thump Janet got aboard: her round pale face glimmered behind the streaky glass, but more clearly reflected Helen saw herself, laughing and waving goodbye. There you are, cheeky, she said to herself: would it hurt you to be nice to Janet? Even to do what she suggests, once in a while? But that path led to the grey swamp of caution and common sense where Janet lived with her elderly parents, weighing every action, debating every word. And from that, Lord preserve me always, Helen said. Only I could say, 'What a good idea, Janet'; yes, tomorrow.

Shadows were teeming black in the long grey street.

Funny what a difference an hour made. Last night she had walked along here in a warm late evening, sky far and blue overhead, bright still from the invisibly westering sun. Tonight; tonight it was night. The drained sky shone bleak and dull in its slot between the leaning chimney-heads. The broken tenements stood up like walls of dream. Her quick feet tacked on the hollow street and the clangour rang raggedly back from closes and boarded shopfronts. She was walking fast, very fast. Her throat was drily sore and her heart unevenly banged. Steady, Helen, she said.

She made a deliberate effort to slow down. What's this, eh? You walked this street last night. The dreaded Claggans? We've disposed of the dreaded Claggans. Nothing is going to happen. Nothing happened last night.

But tonight had a different smell.

Scurries among the broken walls that could have been cats or rats. She turned her eyes sideways, not moving her head. The street-lamps gave less light than she remembered; many were broken; for a hundred-yard stretch they were all out, and she moved through an underworld of swimming dusk. She came into the orbit of the next light with a hiccup of relief. But it was a pale light, a corpse-light, uncomforting: and beyond it the shadows crowded in.

She thought she heard a step behind.

She jerked round, puppet-pulled by terror; but there was no one there, the canyon of grey cliff houses stretching empty, diced with shadow. A cat, questing on hind legs, nudged an abandoned dustbin, and there was the sound she had heard. Silly, how silly. Now Helen, take a grip. Half-way there.

She flung up her head and marched on. The street made its expected oblique bend, the houses crowded closer together, and here again the lights were smashed and dead. She came out of the brief deep darkness shaking, a sob in her throat. Ah God, only half-way there, as far again to go. On her left, straight and short, the alley she had seen last night ran innocently to the main road.

Lights, buses, people, noise, all she wanted was there. It was still, the alley, and sunk in the queer twilight of the long Claggans evening: two antique gas-lamps high up on the walls leaked a sucked-lemon light. But it was a short cut. Fifty yards to the lights and the people. Fifty, sixty steps perhaps. She would count them. She turned into the alley, counting and walking fast.

On the count of fifteen he came out of the shadows more silently than the slinking cats.

He had an old piece of sacking in his hands. He was proud of this idea: he had had such trouble, after the first one, with the splattered blood. The sacking went soft and harsh over her head, smothering the screams, and in the same instant he swung her round by her pinned arms to crash her skull against the high brick wall. One blow was enough to silence her, but he went on. 'Bitch, bitch, bitch,' he was saying intently as he beat. Not the bitch who had crossed him, but like enough, with her proud walk and her long blonde hair: like enough, she would do. There was an old shed nearby. After he had pulled her inside, the alley was quiet again, except for the scutter of a rat. Brady's lame foot made only a slight dragging rustle as he crept away, not so loud as the drag of the girl's sandals in the bloody dust. Outside the shadows it was still light enough, the bonny long summer Claggans evening, God curse it: he knew what he had seen. At the corner of the alley he had to vomit, but in his deadly fear he did not even stop for that. He dragged himself on, and retched, and sobbed.

Perhaps that was what the murderer heard. He heard something, anyway, as he came out of the shed, which made him look back into the darkness and hurry away. He did not even notice that he had left the blood-sodden sacking trailing half out of the shed door. He moved altogether more quickly and less carefully than was his habit; he was actually running as he crossed the back-courts, which was most unusual in a cool, well-organized person like Quinn.

Thursday

1

Kieron opened the door dressed in trousers and shirt, but looking as if he had slept in them. Mrs Sheehan whispered humbly, 'Am I too early for ye?' She felt a bit daft, standing there on the landing with a fistful of money.

'Not a bit,' said Kieron. 'Coming in?' He held the door open: the house was dankly cold, somebody's shirt was draped on the hallstand, and to the usual heavy, unaired atmosphere was added a faint smell of vomit. She said, 'Thanks, Kieron,' and stepped inside.

'Danny's away out for the milk,' said Kieron. 'We a' slept in. It would be past twelve before I got in, an' the old fella was just behind me. God, the state he was in this time. We had to hose him down.'

'I shouldny have woke you,' said Mrs Sheehan.

'Damn the bit o' that. I've to get to my work anyway,' said Kieron cheerfully. 'Listen, I was that late last night I got the morning paper. A' the runners an' the prices.' He pulled out the racing section and spread it on the cluttered table, moving aside a cracked cup and half a pound of margarine.

'But I've picked ma fancy,' said Mrs Sheehan. 'Wait till ye hear the name! It's called Country Cottage. Canny lose, can it?'

'Well, it's no' the favourite, I know that,' said Kieron doubtfully. His finger travelled down the race-card. 'Here ye are. Aw, God, Mrs Sheehan, it's fifty to one. Ye might have picked one with a' its faculties.'

'Fifty to one!' She might have been listening to a prophecy. 'It's meant, so it is. Listen though, Kieron, have I got it right? At fifty to one, say it wins, I'd get ma five hundred pounds?'

'No,' said Kieron with a tolerant smile. 'No' unless you put on ten. Then ye'd get—'

'Did I no' tell you?' said Mrs Sheehan. 'It's ten I want ye to lay for me.'

Kieron stared at her in consternation.

'Ma bingo tenner,' said Mrs Sheehan. She smoothed out the

two five-pound notes on top of the newspaper between them.

'Oh my God, Mrs Sheehan,' said Kieron, staring at the notes, 'I couldny dae that. That's real money you're throwing down the siver.'

'It's bingo money,' Mrs Sheehan corrected him. 'I'll never miss it. By rights I shouldny have it.'

'Aye, but give yourself a chance!' cried Kieron. 'You don't need to get the whole five hundred on one race, do ye? Pick a horse at a decent price. Back it each way.'

'Even if it was the favourite, it still could come in last, could it no'?'

'Oh sure,' said Kieron in despair. 'It could take a heart attack. Likely they a' will except Country Cottage.'

Mrs Sheehan laughed. 'Cheer up, son. Ye'll be right, I'm sure.' She rolled up the two five-pound notes and pushed them into his hand. 'But ma fancy's Country Cottage an' I'm backing it to win. At fifty to one.'

Danny, his arms occupied with a loaf and two bottles of milk, came in backwards, giving the door a hearty butt. He grinned at them silently, for he was carrying a folded newspaper between his teeth.

'Oh Danny, sorry, son,' said Kieron. 'I forgot to tell you I got a paper.'

'It'll no' be this one,' said Danny, dropping it on to the table. 'This is just out.'

Kieron turned it over and the headline stood clear: 'lucky murderer strikes again.'

'Mother o' God,' said Mrs Sheehan. 'No' another young lassie.' She bent over the paper and of its own accord her hand moved in the sign of the cross.

'"The sound of running feet",' she read slowly, '"alarmed residents of Claggans shortly before midnight. Police found a piece of blood-soaked material in an alleyway, and the discovery led to . . ."' Her face twisted and she turned the page.

'Her heid was a' bashed in,' said Danny with gusto. Nobody checked him.

'A school lassie,' said Mrs Sheehan pitifully. 'Just finished her sixth year. Ah, God, they'll need to get him.'

'She'd been in the Gogo,' said Kieron, reading, 'her an' her pal. But no' local lassies, see. God, I wonder if I seen them. There was two lassies at the window table last night. I wouldny have noticed them only for their pan-loaf voices.'

Helen's young face, an expressionless snippet from an old photograph, looked out gravely from the smudged newsprint. Beside her stared Janet, pale and fat and ugly in grief. "I left her only minutes before," said her weeping friend. "We had come down to the Claggans to make arrangements for a folk-song concert in aid of charity. Everything was arranged. It will never take place now."'

'Sounds as if she cares more about the concert,' said Kieron; but Mrs Sheehan shook her head. She knew about the silly things you say, the unimportant thoughts that had been whirling in the poor lassie's shocked mind, in face of the blank forever wall of death.

A connection could not be ruled out, said the paper cautiously in quotation, between this murder and the two previous Claggans killings. Another police spokesman, apparently, had said 'This murderer, if it is the same man, has had luck on his side so far. He strikes in comparatively broad daylight, a stone's throw from busy streets.' It was all unusually expansive, coming from the police: for once you could sense, behind the uniforms and the quotes, the real anger and shock.

"'Any number of passers-by might have seen him —'"

"Aye,' said Kieron, with his mouth set. 'Such as me an' my da. We must have been skiting about between this an' the Gogo half the night. I walked five mile if I walked a yard.'

"— but so far no eye-witnesses have come forward,"' read Mrs Sheehan. "'Anyone who may have seen a running man —'"

They'll see one in a minute,' said Kieron. The frown that put years on him was back between his brows. 'Never heed breakfast for me, Danny. I'll need to get down that road like the clappers.'

'You'll not run very far like that,' said Mrs Sheehan as he limped towards the door. 'What did you do to your foot?'

'I've a blister the size o' Queen Street Station,' said Kieron, 'and I couldny run a temperature—'

He stopped abruptly. Mrs Sheehan, reading over the headlines once more in a private wake for the young blonde girl, looked up in surprise. He said, "This man that ran through the back-courts. Was he the murderer?"

'Well, ye know how they never say. But they want to find him anyway.' She paused: there was an odd pity in her voice as she said, 'It must have been a desperate kind o' running.'

Kieron let out his breath in a huge sigh. He was hidden from Danny for the moment by the heavy front door. In the grey light of the stairhead Mrs Sheehan saw him pass his hand across his face. 'Did ye ever see my da running?' he said.

Brady was fast asleep in the room, but he crossed the landing before them with his painful crab-like step.

Mrs Sheehan said matter-of-factly, 'Well, sure God's good. Didn't I tell you ye'd nothing to worry about?'

'You did,' said Kieron. He snatched his jacket off a peg and slung it over his shoulder. 'I'll get you a winner the day, Mrs Sheehan, if I have to get up there an' ride it myself.'

'Sure if you did how could it lose?' said Mrs Sheehan with love: and Kieron grabbed her and smacked a kiss on her delicate fat cheek. Danny, coming out of the kitchen, nearly dropped the teapot.

2

Wee John, wearing only his nappy, kicked in his drawer, and Bernie, in her slip, moved slowly about the kitchen, getting together a salad for tea. The lettuce was small and limp, the tomatoes hard and pale. 'Your granny telt us,' she said to the baby, 'to get the salad things going to the park, afore the best got sold. How could you no' have reminded me?' He laughed, adoring her. She swooped on him, picked him up and danced him round the kitchen. It was one of the moments when it seemed quite a good idea, a baby in the house.

'Ach, but John, your granny'll be in on top of us,' she said. This was Mrs Agnew's day, out in Giffnock, so that her mother would be later than usual, but still the time was going on. The baby chuckled when she put him back in the drawer: he was a good wee soul, really. Her mother said, laughing, 'Wait till he starts his teeth.'

Then there would be the thing about getting him out of nappies. Then he would get chicken-pox and whooping-cough from the kids in the street. Then he would go to school and get everything else. Bernie scowled at him and he squealed with delight. 'You'll have me tied till I'm forty, ye wee bugger,' she said.

By that time she would be fat and happy like her mother. God, no, she didn't see it. She washed lettuce, cut up tomatoes, boiled eggs, sliced radishes; spangled pictures reeled out in her mind. Miss Bernadette Sheehan jet-setting to Paris and New York, Miss Bernadette Sheehan at the Royal Command Performance. And then there was the husband smoking his pipe in the study, three lovely children who'd managed to get themselves out of nappies and through measles on their own, all in a ranch-type house in the country with two acres of garden —

'Oh my God,' said Bernie, 'Mammy's race.'

She ran to the ancient wireless set, turned it on and thumped it. Pop music crashed and twittered as she spun up and down the wave-band. 'Oh Mammy,' she cried over her shoulder, for the front door had opened, 'I missed the racing results.'

'Never mind, hen,' said Mrs Sheehan, leaning on the doorpost to get her breath after the stairs. 'I got a paper at the corner.'

Bernie, kneeling by the wireless, turned round, big-eyed, a hand at her heart.

'I haveny read it yet,' said Mrs Sheehan with a gasping laugh. 'I thought I'd wait an' read it with you.'

'Oh, Mammy!' Not in a hundred years could Bernie have done that, but of course it was twice the fun. Mrs Sheehan sank sighing into the big chair: Bernie knelt beside her and helped her open out the paper. 'Start from the back,' she breathed.

There were no results on the back page, though plenty of forecasts, none of them tipping Country Cottage. 'Kieron didny think much of it,' nodded Mrs Sheehan. Next page, football. Next, athletics. Next—

'It'll no' be among the small ads, surely,' said Bernie.

They leafed through to the front page: Bernie sat back on her heels, disgusted. 'Bloody fivepence down the stank,' she said.

But Mrs Sheehan was calm. 'We're daft, Bernie,' she said. 'It'll be in the stop press.' She turned the paper sideways, and there it was. Country Cottage had won the big race at fifty to one.

Bernie began to giggle, and went on till her mother had to give her a shake. Mrs Sheehan herself was quite calm. 'What's the matter, Bernie?' she kept saying. 'Sure I told you it would win.'

'We'll need to celebrate,' choked Bernie. 'I'll go out for some beer.'

She snatched up a shopping-bag and was half-way to the door before her mother said, 'If I was you, Bernie, I'd put on a frock.'

She came back with half-a-dozen cans of beer. Kieron wasn't in yet; she went across the landing to invite Danny, but he said in a loud whisper that he was staying in to make his da's tea. Even Bernie in her excitement could see why. Brady was crouched by the empty grate with a blanket over his shoulders: overnight he had aged ten years and shrunk to half his size.

'What's up with Mr Brady in God's name?' she said, rather shaken, when she went back into their festive house.

'Ah, he was as sick as a dog last night,' said Mrs Sheehan, her brows puckered. 'Sure it's bound to happen with the stuff he takes on board. He's his own worst enemy, poor Pat.'

Bernie got giggly again over the beer and salad. She kept saying, 'Mammy, it's no' true, is it? Five hundred pounds? You haveny really won it, have ye?' Mrs Sheehan smiled, turning the beer-mug between her hands. 'I just knew,' she said. 'Country Cottage. It couldny lose.'

"When will you go and see about your wee house?"

'Tomorrow,' Mrs Sheehan said. 'I wonder what would be the best way to do it. I'll maybe go and see Annie's James. He knows about that sort o' thing.'

After another can of beer Bernie was saying, 'You'll get using your new rag rug after all. Mammy, honest, I thought it would be wore out afore you got a cottage.'

'It'll look great by the fireside,' said Mrs Sheehan. 'Do you know what I've a notion for, Bernie? You're no' to laugh. A rocking-chair. I mind we had one at Strathblane.'

Later still she said, 'Bernie, I couldny have flitted to a high flat, do ye know that? I never said to nobody, but I couldny stick yon.

The lifts for one thing.'

'In London,' said Bernie, 'I was once in a lift that broke down. They had to haul us out the top.'

'Oh, ma wee lamb.'

'It was a great giggle,' said Bernie.

'It would be a bigger yin,' said Mrs Sheehan, 'if it was me they were hauling out,' and they drank to that. Bernie said, 'Mammy, you can tell them where to put their high flats now,' and they drank to that too. Half-an-hour later Mrs Sheehan was saying, 'Ye've no idea, Bernie, what it's like first thing in the morning. Ah, it's fresh an' cool. I used to feed the hens when I was a wee lassie. Funny, I'd forgot that till yon day on the bus from Annie's. There was a red sky, Bernie, like a rose, an' snow on the hills.'

The cupboard door swung open wide and out it all came. Scuffing up the white soft dust behind the cows' rocking rumps, at milking-time, coming home. Closing fat hands round a baby chicken soft and yellow as wee John's hair — 'An' the laugh was, Bernie, they were a' covered wi' mites. You should have heard me roaring till my da came an' picked them off me.' And running on the hill in the fresh morning. Running, running. 'I'm daft though, Bernie. I'm past the running, had I twenty wee houses. But John,' she said, 'he'll run on the grass.'

She was quiet. Had she said too much? No, it was safe to say it all now, to open the cupboard door and throw away the key that she had turned with tears as a lassie in a Claggans set-in bed. 'Dinny think they haveny been good years, Bernie,' she said. 'They've been good an' they've been bad. But yon day on the bus, some way, I kent they were done.'

Bernie said, 'What's the time, Mammy?'

'Clock's stopped," said Mrs Sheehan. 'What would you say?'

'That's the thing,' said Bernie, 'I make it seven o'clock, but it canny be that.'

'No, no,' said Mrs Sheehan. 'Kieron gets in about six.'

The first zest of celebration had faded somehow. They cleared the table, took the beer-cans to the midden; Bernie peered at her watch again and shook it, but it was ticking truthfully. The time was twenty-past seven.

'He'll be having a wee celebration for us,' said Mrs Sheehan confidently.

'He might let ye have the money first.'

'Ah, that's safe enough.'

'If it was anyone but Kieron I would wonder,' said Bernie.

'Now, Bernie,' said Mrs Sheehan. 'I think I hear him coming.'

But there were three men coming up the stairs. They staggered in unequal partnership, and the two strangers had Kieron's arms hitched round their necks.

'Is this where he stays, missis?' said the smaller of the two, distinctly aggrieved. 'We'd a hell o'' a job getting him to tell us.'

'Aye,' said Mrs Sheehan, 'bring him in.' They slung Kieron into the big chair, where he sat with his head in his hands. 'Thanks, boys,' she said. 'But how in the name o' God has he done it by this time o' day?'

'It's no' our blame,' began the smaller.

His friend said, 'We just went in for a hauf after work, missis, but he started drinking doubles like they was lemonade.'

'God,' said the annoyed small one, 'we thought we'd be there till the New Year.'

Mrs Sheehan and Bernie hardly noticed the men go. They stood and looked at Kieron, who groaned a little as if their gaze hurt him. His face was the colour of old whitewash, black hair streaked across it like mud.

'Mammy,' said Bernie, 'I think he's drank your money.'

'Whisky's a terrible price,' said Mrs Sheehan, 'but he canny have drank five hundred pounds since five o'clock?'

'No, no,' said Bernie, 'your stake. He's kept it and drank that.'

'He wouldny do that.' Mrs Sheehan put her hands on his shoulders and eased him back in the chair. He said with closed eyes, 'I'm no' going home. Leave me alone. Go an' —'

'Aye, well,' said Mrs Sheehan, 'here ye are. What happened, eh?'

Kieron opened his eyes and shut them again, with a violent shudder, when he saw Mrs Sheehan. 'Oh Christ,' he said. 'I didny want to come home.'

'Ah, Kieron,' said Mrs Sheehan, 'don't worry yourself now. Did ye forget to put the money on?' He made an indistinct reply. 'Never heed, son. Sure you've more to do than run messages for me.'

Kieron shook his head slowly. 'Fella,' he said, 'that gave me Rags to Riches.'

'Aye,' said Mrs Sheehan. She appeared to know what he was going to say.

'Fella said Methuselah's Father,' said Kieron. 'Great tip. Great price.' He grabbed Mrs Sheehan's hand. 'I couldny let you lose a' that money,' he said. 'Aw, Mrs Sheehan, I was so sure yours hadny a chance.'

Bernie began, 'Ye silly —' but her mother cut in sharply. 'So ye backed the sure thing for me,' she said. "That was a kind thought, Kieron.'

'An' I lost ye—'

'I told ye,' said Mrs Sheehan, 'it was only bingo money.'

Kieron shook his head again. 'No,' he said. 'No, no. I lost ye your wee house.'

The agony in his voice reached Bernie as she stood awkwardly beside her mother. She saw tears in his eyes. She envied the sure gentleness of her mother's big hand, fondling his rough dark head.

'Ah, Kieron,' her mother said, 'you was trying to help. That's a' that matters, son.'

With his head still bent, blinking fast, he dug in his pocket and pulled out a handful of silver. 'That's a' I've got,' he said. 'Will ye wait till tomorrow?'

Mrs Sheehan hesitated only for a moment. Her hands cupped under his and she took the few coins. 'That's real nice o' you, Kieron,' she said, 'but that's a' you're to give me. I'll take this an' see can I still get into the bingo. Sure my luck's running strong.'

He tried to smile, but that was his effort made. His head went down on his arms.

Her mother drew Bernie into the lobby. 'Hours he's been screwing himself up to face me,' she said. 'Give him a minute. He'll be all right.'

'I'il make some coffee, will I?' said Bernie.

'It aye helps,' said Mrs Sheehan. She bit her lips. 'I'd better go to the bingo right enough, Bernie. It'll vex him the more every time he sees me.'

'Later on,' Bernie said, 'he'll maybe feel like eating something.'

'I wouldny be surprised,' her mother said. 'You give him what he wants.'

Bernie went back into the kitchen and lit the noisy gas under the kettle. Kieron was sitting up, almost back to normal except for his white face and black-smudged eye-sockets. She moved from stove to sink and cupboard to table, and did not know what she was doing.

'Bernie,' he said, slurring it, 'I could kill myself.'

'Oh, I wouldny do that, Kieron,' she said. It was easy enough to comfort Danny: you opened your arms and he put his head on your heart. Funny the difference they made, those few years between the boys.

'I wouldny have done that for the world,' he said, 'no' to your mammy.' He was shivering now: Bernie told herself he needed the coffee. The kettle began to sing. 'Mammy doesny mind,' she said. 'She told you, didn't she?'

'Aye, but —' He lifted his head. She was kneeling beside him now: her thin hands on the arm of the chair were trembling a little too. 'Bernie,' he said. It was no different from comforting Danny after all. She put her arms round him and he buried his face between her breasts. It was nothing like comforting Danny. It was what she was born to do.

When Mrs Sheehan came back from the bingo Danny was on the landing, biting his nails, veering uncertainly between his door and hers.

'Is your da all right, Danny?'

'Oh aye. He's gone to bed.' Danny glanced over at her closed door. 'I was wondering if wee John's all right, but. He's been crying an' crying.'

'Crying?' said Mrs Sheehan. 'I wonder did Bernie slip out for a message? You didn't look in on him, did you?'

'I tried,' said Danny, 'but the door's snibbed.'

'Oh, son, it's never snibbed.' But as she spoke she heard, soft but clear, the sound of the snib being very gently slipped back.

Bernie was picking up wee John; Kieron was leaning on the mantelpiece. They said in unison, 'Well, you're back.' They stopped and giggled and looked at each other. Kieron said 'Snowball tonight?'

'No' a ha'penny,' said Mrs Sheehan. Bernie bent her head over wee John and gave him a smacking kiss.

Danny said sternly, 'Is he all right ? He was crying an' —'

'Funny,' said Bernie with her lovely smile. 'I didny hear him.'

Friday

1

Lisa, going in to start the long one-to-eight duty that dragged so on a summer day, met Quinn coming out of the library. For a moment she thought he didn't know her. His eyes were wide open, almost fixed; but then of course the glaring bright noontime street must be reflecting light in his face. 'Hello, Quinn,' she said shyly.

He paused on the steps and relaxed his hard stare. 'Hello, Lisa,' he said. No more than that; but he stopped, and they stood in the heavy shade of the entrance. She hadn't seen him since he had stormed out of the reading-room. What was the proper thing to do now?

She stood awkwardly before him, twisting her cotton gloves in her hot hands. Was it her place to apologize? Clumsy Lisa, so miserably lacking in finesse. But then (a nagging voice in her mind insisted) ridiculous Quinn, to take such instant and deep offence. For forty-eight hours she had swung from one to the other point of view. It was last night that she had passed through a zone of vague uneasiness: such a sudden, such a violent huff . . . ?

But he was standing with her pleasantly enough now, and his unexpectedly cultured voice, one of the first good things she had noticed about him, talked quietly of this and that. Surely he was offering her another chance?

Quinn talked quietly, but not of what filled his mind. The blonde hair, the fair face. Soft between his hands, heavy and soft afterwards among the sharp-edged bricks and rusty iron. Lisa, you would be surprised, surprised, surprised, if you knew what I am thinking now.

He swallowed the saliva and opened his eyes wide. The, silly bitch was saying, 'I didn't see you in the library yesterday, Quinn. Did you come in?'

'No,' he said, debonair again. 'I slept in yesterday.' That was true: for some reason it always followed. 'Kept me back all day.'

'Ah,' she said. She lowered her head and twiddled the fingers of her clean white gloves. Of course it had been her fault entirely, he said to himself: no blame attached to Quinn. Now had she been punished enough? He could feel no particular pull one way or the other. Perhaps it should depend on what she said next. Two old men came hobbling up the library steps, and Quinn drew aside, though not very much, to let them pass.

In the dim entrance hall, as they stopped for a last drag before entering the smokeless zone, old Moses said to Mad Mac, 'I've thought who he minds me o'. That young fella that kept daein' lassies in.'

'Manuel do ye mean?' said Mad Mac.

'No, no,' said Moses, his clever dark eyes snapping impatiently. 'No' Manuel. Jack the Ripper.'

Mac thought it over with care. 'He canny mind you o' him,' he said at last. 'You never seen Jack the Ripper. That was in the olden days.'

'Aw God,' said Moses in exasperation. 'Would it help if I telt ye I was the Wandering Jew?'

'You're a blasphemous old bastard so ye are, Moses,' said Mad Mac uncertainly. Moses laughed and flattened his fag-end on the sole of his shoe, and they went into the reading-room. They half expected to see Pat Brady, but he wasn't there. Nobody had seen him about since Wednesday night.

Lisa let Quinn talk: the reverse of usual, this was, but then he wasn't quite his usual self today. For whatever reason, there was an excitement, an urgency in him that she had not felt before. Oh, it would be such a pity if they didn't make up. He said something about the weather: the air was heavier today, humid, as if the heat-wave might be on the way out. It was, anyway, an opening for her.

'I hope it keeps dry tonight,' she said. 'It's my late night and I haven't got a coat.' She gave a little twitch of her unprotected shoulders in the low-cut summer dress.

She thought he wasn't going to take it up: but he said, 'When do you finish?'

She raised her head, determined, hopeful. 'Eight o'clock,' she said. The pale-blue eyes met hers directly. It had worked after all.

'I'll be here to pick you up,' he said without even a smile; and she said, 'All right, Quinn.'

All right, indeed, he thought, you little hag. His calm surface voice went on talking of this and that, and the deep fury inside him was sleeping, sated for the time. But really, my dear, you must learn you can't do just what you like with Quinn. Tonight, yes, well, we'll see how you behave.

'See you later, then?' he said.

'Yes, Quinn. We could go for coffee or something, perhaps.'

'Something like that,' he said, smiling goodbye.

2

Danny was washing up, singing a little song to himself at the sink. He was quick to pick up a mood from people he loved, and Kieron, shaving in front of the cracked mirror, was cheerful tonight. He was going out with Bernie.

Brady was the skeleton at the feast. For a day and a half he had been uncannily quiet, crouching over the hearth, jumping every time one of the boys came through the door. That had worn off a little, and he had ventured out in the afternoon for another shot of whatever it was he had taken to drinking. He was back at the fireside now, and the drink had taken over. The terrified horror, told to no one, was still there coiled at the back of his mind, but surging to the fore came the general tide of his grievances. 'If you kent what I ken,' he muttered, 'you'd be mair civil tae an old man.'

'What the hell's the matter now, Da?' said Kieron, tying his tie. He was in the sunniest of moods and not inclined to quarrel with anyone.

'Whatsa matter? None of yez is ever in this bloody house,' said Brady, 'that's whatsa matter.'

'We're both in now,' said Kieron reasonably. 'Sure we a' had our tea together. Is that no' what you're aye greeting about?'

'Aye, sure,' said Brady. 'An' there ye are tailing yerself up like a fancy boy. It's no' to stay in wi' your old faither, is it?'

'Danny's staying in.'

'That's fine,' Brady said. 'He looks after the old fella an' you go out wi' your—'

Kieron said, still quite pleasantly, 'Shut it, Da.'

'Ye see!' cried Brady. 'Gi'e them the best years o' your life an' they turn an' swear at ye!' He pushed himself to his feet, holding on to the arms of the chair. 'Who's the heid o' this hoose?'

'God help us,' said Kieron, 'you are, Da, an' ye're welcome to it. Sit down now, will you?'

'If I am,' said Brady, lowering his head and staring from Kieron to Danny, 'there's to be some changes made around here. Startin' wi' you, ye jumped-up hoorin' wee bastard.'

Kieron bit hard on his tongue, because it was time he was across calling for Bernie. He turned away and went into the lobby for his jacket; but Danny, twisting the dish-towel in his big hands, cried shrilly, 'You've no' to speak like that to Kieron!'

Kieron in the lobby jerked up his head: for a moment he was a wee boy again, back in the bad days before Brady went away, hearing through a closed door the panting and thudding and heaving, the hoarse muttering, the swish and slap. With one arm in his jacket he flung himself back into the kitchen: and it was right enough, Danny was getting a hammering. He had fallen on his knees by the sink, his arms flung up to cover his head, and Brady, the belt twisted round his fist, was slashing like a hangman. But it wasn't hurting Danny. Brady was wild and desperate and weak. Not one blow in six came anywhere near connecting with Danny's broad bowed shoulders, and the odd one that landed was harmless as a tissue streamer's flick.

Kieron, not even using his hands, elbowed his father aside. Brady lurched and the windmilling belt smacked, for once quite sharply, across the side of Kieron's face; Kieron shook his head and went down on one knee beside Danny. Because the alarming thing was Danny, huddled on the floor. There was nothing frightening about Brady and his belt: you might laugh at him, you might cry. A child of five could have pushed him aside and walked away. But Danny was curled up on the cold dirty linoleum like a stillborn lamb.

'That'll larn ye,' panted Brady. 'Now for Lord Muck.'

Kieron said almost absently, 'Hit me an' I'll swing for ye.' He helped Danny up. Danny stood limply, shoulders a little hunched, hands hanging. 'Get a grip on yourself,' Kieron said. 'He never touched you. Are ye all right?'

Danny blinked and nodded. Some life returned to his face: stiffly, like a carved doll, he turned his large luminous eyes on Kieron. 'I telt him, Kieron,' he said, 'sure I did?'

Brady, still panting, was swinging his belt in random circles. 'I'm the boss here!' he gasped.

'Aye, sure,' said Kieron, 'you're the bloody Aga Khan. Right, Danny. Never heed him. You dropped your dishcloth.'

Brady, ignored, deflated quickly. He sank back into his chair and said, 'Hell o' a thing.'

Kieron looked at him for a moment, and gave it up. 'As long as ye're feeling better,' he said, and began to pull on his jacket again.

'In God's name who'd hae sons?' said Brady to the fireplace, becoming tearful. 'One o' them a cursin' swearin' hoorin' bastard an' the other a bloody halfwit.'

It was like a douche of cold water over Kieron. He gasped and jerked round to look at Danny: but Danny, morosely drying off the rest of the dishes, did not seem to have heard. God, he mustn't have heard. Kieron looked back at his father, sitting there snuffling in the hearth; and the red old eyes said, Why not?

And why not? None of them had been picking their words these past few weeks. What he called Brady, what Brady called him, slipped off them both like oil. But calling Danny that was like shouting after a cripple. The bucketful of cold water was trickling down Kieron's spine, each drop a doubt, a fear from the past. Nobody must ever call Danny a halfwit, because it was too nearly true.

Danny turned from the sink to give Kieron his wide, infinitely trusting smile.

'You'll be late for Bernie, Kieron,' he said.

Kieron slammed out of the house without saying goodbye.

He stood for a moment on the landing, biting his lips, hardly knowing why he was there: but Bernie slipped out of the house opposite, warm and sweet as she had been last night. He gripped her round the shoulders, taking a fierce comfort from the delicate flesh and bone, and ran her downstairs.

'What's up, Kieron?' He swung her into the angle of two ruined walls and pressed her back against the stone. Her slim hand came up, unalarmed, and traced the line of his cheekbone with a butterfly touch. 'Is that a black eye you've got?' she said.

'The old bugger,' said Kieron. He felt that dangerous, hysterical laughter coming on. 'He must have landed me one after all.' He put his hand up to his face: Bernie stood on her tiptoes and pressed against him, all her slim warm length. 'Oh, Bernie,' he said. 'We had a hell o' a set-to there again.'

'Will I get mammy to help?'

For a moment it was a temptation, to give up like a wee boy, to fall back gratefully into the days when there was nothing your mammy couldn't do. But 'It's no' like that this time,' he said. 'It's —' It wasn't what Brady had done, the weak violence of misery guttering out as soon as it flared; it wasn't anything particular he had said. Kieron looked back down the months to Holy Thursday, and everything was hopelessly clear. 'I think my da's off his head,' he said.

'It's maybe just the wine,' said Bernie eagerly.

He had to laugh at that for comfort: but she was trying to help, her big eyes dark with the effort. 'It's Danny too,' he said. But that he couldn't tell even Bernie, not yet. Only he knew where the sun rose and set for Danny, and the knowledge was too much. 'Bernie,' he said, 'I canny carry on much longer.'

'Ah Kieron, it's surely not as bad as that.'

'I canny see what to do,' he said. Get Brady into hospital? They could cure him, maybe, but he'd never forgive the one who put him there. See Danny's teachers? He couldn't really be daft, he'd stuck it somehow at school; they liked him, of course, nobody could help liking Danny. But never in God's creation could you imagine him holding down a job. And he was nearly fifteen. 'It's time I need, Bernie,' said Kieron, 'time to think. But I have to go back in there, an' it's getting worse every day.'

She held him, her fingers linked in the soft dark hair at the back of his neck. He stared down at her, his brows knitted in that worried way he had, almost puzzled. He might hardly know it himself, but he was asking her for help. She could help, she could give him comfort and he would forget for a while; but only for a while.

Holding him close, for a blink of time she saw what he was seeing. The grey decaying Claggans: they even had to kiss between two broken walls, their lips dry with the hot summer dust. The sad, dirty house, and in it the old man and Danny, his burden for ever, no way (because he was Kieron) to put it down.

He bent his head to the sharp sweet peaks of her collarbone, and an unexpected breeze of evening, coming up from the docks, whirled the dust at their feet. She was back inside her own head, and it was all quite simple.

'You need to get away, Kieron,' she said. 'Just for a week-end.' He raised his head, startled but not angry, with a kind of unbelieving hope. 'It'll a' look different,' she said, 'once you're away from it. Let's go to London.'

'You an' me?' he said stupidly.

She nodded, bright-eyed. 'Just the two nights. I know plenty of places we could stay. Could we no', Kieron?' She stood on tiptoe again and her mouth was gentle on his bruised face. 'Would you not like that?' she said.

She was wonderful. She knew what he needed, when he hardly knew it himself. A week-end away, clear of it all. He put his palms against the rough stone wall, looking down at her between his arms. Her green eyes were open and candid. 'We could get the overnight bus,' she whispered. 'It's no' that dear.'

'Pay-day,' he said, I'd manage right enough.' Her long mouth began to curve in a smile. 'But Bernie,' he said, 'what about the baby?'

'Sure my mammy loves looking after him. A couple o' days, she'll no' mind that.'

But that was a mistake: Kieron drew back. 'Ah, Bernie, we canny do it. Can you see us telling your mammy we're away for the week-end?'

'She couldny say naethin', for God's sake, we're no' weans.'

'That's no' the point,' said Kieron.

'Suppose no',' said Bernie a little sulkily. She thought, and gleamed with an idea. 'Listen! She's awful fond o' Danny. We'll tell him to tell her. But no' till we're away.'

'He'd never remember,' said Kieron gloomily.

'He will if we promise him something,' said the realistic Bernie. They conspired, whispering, close in each other's arms behind the crumbling wall.

'I'll run up an' tell him then,' said Kieron, 'an' get the money.'

'I'll pick up a few things. I can tell Mammy I'm back for my coat.'

'When does the bus go?'

'Oh, late, I'm no' sure. We can go somewhere first. The Gogo maybe.'

'Only one thing about the Gogo.'

'What's that?'

'Too many folk.'

They kissed long and hard in the shadow of the ruins.

'Just in for my coat, Ma,' called Bernie, running through the lobby.

'Is it no' so warm, hen?'

'Might even rain.' Oddly enough this was true: the limpid sky of the past week was bunchy with clouds: a dampness hung in the air. Bernie pulled on her coat, put a toothbrush in the pocket, rolled up a nylon nightie and stuffed it in her handbag. Not that it mattered, but she liked to look nice. She smiled to herself as she moved quickly round the room, picking up this and that, in case they might happen to stay a bit longer.

Kieron took his money from the locked drawer and stowed it in his inside pocket. There was enough food in the house for the week-end. He considered for a moment, and put two pounds back in the drawer, in case London cleaned him out. He thought he had attended to everything. 'Danny!' he called.

'Aye, Kieron?' Danny bounced in from the other room.

'Will ye do something for me?'

'Sure, Kieron.'

'I don't want ye to do it,' said Kieron carefully, 'till ten o'clock. Can ye tell ten o'clock?'

'Oh aye,' said Danny. 'But the clock's stopped.'

Kieron unbuckled his wristwatch. Take this then. Aye —' as Danny's mouth opened - 'it's to keep, if ye do this right. Now listen, son. Bernie an' me's going away. Just for the weekend,' he added, seeing Danny's chin begin to quiver.

'Where are ye going, Kieron?'

'England,' said Kieron. He knew it was all one to Danny. 'We'll bring ye back something nice. Now Danny, when the watch says ten o'clock, will ye tell Bernie's mammy?'

'I've to tell her ye'll bring me—'

'Aye. No,' said Kieron. He heard the Sheehans' door open and close, and Bernie's light foot on the landing. 'You've to tell her we're away for the weekend. But don't tell her till—'

'Ten o'clock,' nodded Danny.

'That's it!' cried Kieron. In his relief he dug into his pocket and hauled out a handful of change. 'And buy yourself some ice-cream tomorrow, eh?'

He jerked his raincoat off the peg. Brady was standing in the lobby in his filthy old coat, slowly winding his muffler round and round his skinny neck. The old anger and pity and love wrenched Kieron's heart.

'Here,' he said, slipping a pound note from the roll in his pocket. 'Have a drink on me if ye feel like it. God, why would I stop ye?'

He slammed the door on Brady's astonished face.

3

Brady had a good drink on Kieron's pound. It was great to go into a pub again and get something with the taste as well as the kick. He enjoyed it so much that he rationed himself: he stowed the change away in the depths of his layered coats and came out, wiping his mouth, not long before eight o'clock.

He turned by habit into the public library, but it was nearly closing-time. The blonde girl was on duty again. He stood by the reading-slopes and looked at her for a while as she went about clearing up the scattered magazines. When she came near he bent over a paper, sucking his teeth and breathing heavily to show that he was intent on reading, but she did not seem to notice him. She had a lot of eye-shadow on and the frown-lines were nowhere to be seen tonight. She moved quickly, excitedly: from long ago - no, not so bloody long after all —Brady knew the signs. She was going out with her lad.

A hot summer night, and the library was quiet: they were turned out sharp at eight. He was, as usual, last to leave. He heard the blonde girl call, 'Need any help there, Miss Grierson?' and her boss reply, 'No, thanks, Lisa, you go on.' He saw her come out on to the steps and pause in that well-bred way she had, pulling on her little gloves.

Her cotton dress was sleeveless and short: a fine big girl. No, she wasn't Rose. Sarah Sheehan had straightened him out about that. But she was a pretty lassie. A bit on her high horse, but God, that came of being young. Through Brady's muddled mind, warm with Kieron's unexpected kindness and the good drink, passed what might have been a garbled Hail Mary for the blonde lassie and for Rose.

He saw her head turn eagerly from side to side; the faintest quiver of her hopeful big mouth, and he thought for a second the bastard had stood her up; and then out of the green shadows by the park gate stepped a tall fair-haired man. 'Well, Lisa,' the man said, and she said in a laugh of relief, 'Hullo, Quinn.' The man took her arm and they walked into the park.

Brady stood sick and shaking by the library wall.

It was broad daylight again: no mistake, there never had been a chance of a mistake. He might have been back in the alley near the Gogo, seeing the blonde girl and the fair-haired man.

He knew that this was not the same girl, alike as they were; he was not so daft or so drunk as that. But there was no mistake. He knew by the smooth neat movements, by the set of the shining gold head, by the handsome downbent face so dreadfully preoccupied in the alley, that it was the same fair-haired man.

Brady lurched across the road and after them into the park. His lame leg wrenched on the rough path and flame shot through his hip-joint: he stopped, sobbing harshly, only for seconds, but knowing that he was losing precious ground. The man and the girl, tall and long-legged, walked with quick smooth strides. Fifty yards ahead already: he would never catch them up. Yet he hobbled on. It was something just to keep them in sight. Aye, he would keep them in sight till the lassie reached her own front door. Ye may be the Lucky Murderer, ye bastard, he panted, and forced his leg forward over and over in pain; but ye canny kill us both at once.

And they had slowed down. Of course they had: the park on a summer evening was no place to hurry through, not with a lassie like Lisa on your arm, even, Brady supposed, if you were a murderer. The man's tweed sleeve lay across the girl's shoulders. Brady saw the broad flat fingers stroking, teasing, caressing the sun-touched skin of her smooth round arm. He recalled what he had last seen those fingers grip, and dry retching seized him for a moment. He began to run, dragging, hirpling, calling, 'Miss! Miss!'

Lisa did not look round at first: why should she after all? 'Miss!' he cried hoarsely, till she glanced frowning over her shoulder. He waved his arm, flapping the dirty overcoat sleeve, lurching on, only yards behind them now. She stopped and a quick flush came to her high fair face: she caught Quinn's arm and pulled him round for protection. 'Go away,' she whispered, almost voiceless in disgust. 'Do you hear? Go away.' And to Quinn, who strangely enough was saying nothing, 'It's that horrible old man again. Oh, God, Quinn, make him go away.'

'Miss,' Brady said, gasping. 'Lemme talk to you. I got something to tell you, miss.'

Lisa shuddered and pushed Quinn backwards along the path, but Brady followed. They zig-zagged, the three of them, like madly linked dancers, towards the further gate of the park. Brady stretched out his hand, and Lisa with a terrified little scream jerked away. 'Oh, Quinn,' she said, 'get the police!'

Quinn cleared his throat. "Go on,' he said, 'get off now.' He sounded edgy, uneasy: Brady's heart leapt.

'Will ye get the police?' he cried. Quinn said nothing. 'Listen, miss. Don't go wi' him. I can tell you—'

'Go away, you—you filth—' said Quinn.

'Aye, you!' cried Brady recklessly. 'You ken where I seen you!'

Lisa, glancing desperately over her shoulder, saw the park gate and the main road and the blessed square red police box. She left Quinn in his paralysis and ran. She stumbled and sobbed, but she ran: the old man, hobbling after her, was still a few yards behind. She clawed at the door, and, more than she hoped, a surprised policeman looked out.

'Please —' she said. 'It's this old man —he keeps pestering me—'

The policeman sighed, heaved himself out of the box and delicately gripped Brady by the rags of his upper arm. 'Now then, Grandpa,' he said.

'It's no' me you want!' cried Brady. 'It's him! I was trying to tell her-'

The policeman looked at Brady, hunched in his steaming coat: weeping red eyes, toothless mouth, the stench of old drink and the sharpness of tonight's dram. He looked at Lisa, young and blonde and distressed. Claggans with its three murdered girls was only across the park. He tightened his grip. 'I think,' he said, 'we'll maybe get hold of a Panda car and run up to the station, the three of us.'

Lisa gave a deep thankful sob. 'Oh, God,' she said. 'I was walking home with my friend, you see —'

'Some bloody friend—' said Brady.

'Your friend?' said the constable.

'Quinn?' said Lisa, turning back towards the park.

But Quinn had gone.

<h1 style="text-align:center">4</h1>

Hand in hand, like young teenagers, Bernie and Kieron came out of the Gogo at eight o'clock into the warm bath of the thundery evening.

'Who said bring our coats?' panted Bernie.

'You did,' said Kieron. Threads of dark hair clung to her damp face and she pushed them back, laughing, as she melted into his arms. They had spent a silly hour in the Gogo, drunk on coffee and chocolate biscuits, talking and giggling about nothing, pressed knee to knee as close as you could get in the circumstances of two chairs and a table.

Months since Kieron had laughed like that: months maybe, he reminded himself, before he might again. He had to remind himself, because his terrible inescapable problems were showing an alarming tendency to slip his mind entirely. Even the week-end had taken on a different look. Not so much a snatched forty-eight-hour pass away from responsibility, but two long golden days in the lazy south alone with Bernie.

'Here, wait a minute,' he said to the pliant warm girl in his arms. 'It's gonny be crowded on that bus.'

Bernie swam to meet his kiss. Behind his shoulder the tilting Claggans houses reeled and swung. In a flutter of her eyelashes she glimpsed someone standing in the shadows across the street: dead white face, dead black hair: it was that new man, the queer fella, behind the Gogo counter. Cheeky bastard staring there—

But Kieron's arms were hard and his mouth was everywhere, and very soon she no longer saw nor cared about Eugene.

Brothers and sisters didn't kiss like that. Well, in some of his books they did; but he knew it was no use pretending any more. He turned away—they never noticed, blind and deaf in their kiss — and hurried away from the Gogo, away from them, away — if only he could! —from himself. He had been going in to work, of course, but that was forgotten. That, and everything else, was swallowed up in the blaze of the passion which was not, and would never be, for him.

The chequered Claggans opened out before him, but tonight he was the only piece on the board. Head down he went, almost running, up and down streets he did not know, through alleys, across waste ground where the rats started and squalled. He cried a little, since there was nobody to see, stumbling on in his bitterness of soul. He had wished his mother into hospital. He had lusted night and day long after green eyes and white skin. What he had wanted, oh God—

But she was a real girl, I loved her, I could have loved her. All I wanted was the chance; only the chance that other people get. Holy Mary, was it a sin after all? I tried, I did try, said Eugene, and the long cliffs of Claggans streets rayed out dizzily from his blindly walking feet. And what use was any of it at all?

He bumped head-on against something, and looked up with a catch of his breath into a flushed angry face and pale blue eyes mad with fear and rage.

'Where the hell d'you think you're going?' snarled Quinn.

'Sorry,' gasped Eugene. 'Sorry.' He side-stepped, but Quinn, meaning to shoulder past him, stepped the same way.

'Sorry, so sorry—'

Eugene dodged and Quinn, passionately cursing, did the same. He dodged and dodged again. As if tied to him by cords, Quinn followed. Eugene in panic let out a shrill frightened giggle: they were in it now, that dreadful dance of misunderstanding that sometimes seems set to go on for ever. And the awful thing was, Eugene realized as Quinn's fair face darkened and swelled, that the man thought he was doing it on purpose.

'Get out of my way, you bastard —' said Quinn in a high hysterical voice.

He lunged at Eugene, gripped his coat lapels and pushed violently. Eugene went backwards: his heel caught on the broken pavement and his head, snapping back, hit the wall behind him.

That was the sound, that was the feeling, a limp body between his hands and the crunch of skull on stone. Quinn's eyes widened and his mouth opened slightly. He banged Eugene's head on the wall again. He was dimly aware of the splattering blood, and more clearly of a car screeching to a stop beside him; but none of this was enough to stop him now. He beat, and beat, and beat.

The Panda car was on its way to pick up an old drunk molesting a girl. The policemen were out of it almost before it stopped: they were throwing themselves on Quinn while, hair hanging over his blood-flecked face, he was still lost in his mindless rage. When they pulled him off he looked at them vacantly, and then down at the dead man at his feet.

His face twisted in a distortion which they were horrified to recognize as a laugh. He laughed quite madly for a long time, and it was all they could do to get the handcuffs on him.

5

The policeman came to Mrs Sheehan's door just before ten. She had lit the fire, because the heat-wave was on its way out at last: she was sitting in the big chair with the baby on her lap and Danny on the rug at her feet, all warm in their firelit cave. Her first thought, when she heard the knock, was that Mary Lynch's time had come, and she went to the door half expecting to find big Eddie shaking and blubbering himself sober. When she saw the uniform she thought: God forgive me for feeling so happy just now.

'Mrs Sheehan?' the policeman said. 'Can you tell me is there going to be anybody in next door?'

'What's wrong?'

'It's all right, Mrs Sheehan.' He was a middle-aged man; he knew very well the effect his uniform had, unexpectedly at the door at night. 'We've got old Mr Brady in the station, but he's not hurt. We're just trying to notify his family.'

She pressed her hands to her lips. 'There's only the two boys.' One in a million, the policeman thought: she was answering his question first before flying off into anxious enquiries. 'One's here with me, but he's only fourteen. The other lad's out. Danny!' she called. 'Did Kieron say when he'd be back?'

Danny put his head out of the kitchen: he did not see the policeman standing back on the landing. He shook his head, bright-eyed, his mouth tightly screwed up.

'Well, you might tell him when he comes in,' said the policeman. 'We're not holding the old man, but I think they're wanting a word with him when he's slept it off. He wasn't in very good trim before.'

'Is he in trouble?' asked Mrs Sheehan softly.

'There's no charge been made,' said the policeman with official caution. It had been a hectic hour or two at the station, and he wasn't going to start explaining what he didn't understand himself. How one man drunk and disorderly in Claggans Park linked up with another beating someone's brains out five streets away was more than he could make out; but the top brass seemed pretty excited about something. 'Thanks, Mrs Sheehan,' he said.

Mrs Sheehan went back into the warm kitchen, red-glinting in the firelight. Danny was peering at the watch which, she now saw, sat awkwardly on his big-boned wrist. His lips moved as if in a count-down. He looked up brightly.

'Kieron an' Bernie's away to England for the week-end,' he announced.

'Mother o' God,' said Mrs Sheehan, as astounded as Danny could have wished.

Her second emotion was anger: the fly pair they were, leaving the message with Danny. And she knew whose idea that had been. God forgive her, but Bernie could be a right wee bitch.

But nobody could blame Danny, whose smile had widened to ecstasy at the success of his bombshell. 'You might have told me, son,' she only said, 'when the man was asking at the door.'

'Oh I couldny,' explained Danny. 'Kieron said no' to tell till the watch said ten.' He held up his wrist, where the hands stood at a minute past the hour.

Mrs Sheehan sighed. 'That's very good then, son,' she said. 'You done that very well.'

'They're bringing me something nice.'

'Oh aye,' said Mrs Sheehan, sitting down heavily by the fire. 'A wee brother for John.'

'Will they?' said Danny in great excitement.

'No' this week-end,' said Mrs Sheehan. She saw that he was all wound up, his big eyes blinking fast. She laughed to take the strain off, and patted the arm of the chair. 'Come an' sit down again, Danny. This is cosy, eh? Listen, your da's away till tomorrow. Would you like to sleep in Bernie's bed tonight?'

'Oh aye, Mrs Sheehan,' said Danny, delighted.

He slung himself across the chair and began to play with wee John, stroking the soles of the baby's feet till the fat toes curled. Mrs Sheehan looked at the two of them, one as innocent as the other. They needed looking after. Ah, thank God they did.

Thunder muttered far away, behind the hills you saw from the high flats. On the cracked pane the first heavy drops of rain began, and Mrs Sheehan remembered that she had latched the window open in the heat. She put the baby into Danny's arms and went over to the window recess.

The rain came all at once, straight and heavy and clean on the dried-out slates and flags. They darkened and shone, the gutters filled and ran; the rough street gathered puddles and sprang up in swift little tulip-leaves under the lancing rain. And up from the broken houses and crumbling ground of the Claggans came, rank and black, the smell of the wet earth underneath: and Mrs Sheehan was not prepared for it at all.

She stood with her hands on the window-sash and gulped it in. When the cottage dream collapsed she had been quick to tell herself she was a silly old wife; cows and grass and summer dust, my God, pretty pictures daubed up from stories and films. There never had been, she had almost convinced herself, a small Sarah running barefoot on the hill. This raw smell hit her in the wind and told her she was wrong: but she thought it told her more.

She left the streaming window open and went back to the fire, gathering up wee John from Danny's clumsy safe arms. 'Do you know something, Danny?' she said. 'It'll no' run away.'

'Will it no', Mrs Sheehan?' said Danny eagerly, ready to agree.

She chuckled and pulled him down on to the rug at her feet. In the rosy kitchen, in the warm wet night, they were fragilely safe. 'If we got a country cottage, Danny,' she said, 'would ye come and stay with us?'

'Sure, Mrs Sheehan.' He beamed and blinked. 'Dead an' alive place, the country.' You could tell by the very turn of his voice when it was not Danny speaking; and Mrs Sheehan could hear as if Bernie was in the room the deep sweet lazy words he had heard. She said, 'Aye, right, son,' and held his head warmly against her knee.

He yawned enormously and said, 'Do ye know where I'd like to stay, Mrs Sheehan? In a skyscraper.'

'You wouldny, would you, Danny?' she said.

'Aye,' he said sleepily. 'A fella showed me how to work the lift. It was rare fun.'

She looked down with love at the top of his rough head. She laughed a little. 'Well now,' she said. 'You'll need to teach me tomorrow.'

[1] See the Afterword by Moira Burgess for further detail.

Afterword

Moira Burgess

The first notation on page one of the small notebook is the pencilled price, one shilling and sixpence (it's rather a classy notebook with a tweedy red cover) and the second is the date, 27.4.69. Then comes the title, *The Day Before Tomorrow*, which was evidently fixed from an early stage. Unusually, the publisher liked it too.

Then I embark on something recognisable, in today's terms, as a mission statement: *What I want to write is a textured story, with depth as well as length and breadth.* Forty years on, did I manage to do that?

Next I become rather portentous: *Written as it were from the inside out, with minimum of description and writer's-eye omniscience, maximum of letting characters convey meaning by their perceptions and emotions.* No wonder I was such a hit with writers' groups in later years. But this nonsense is recognisable as a writer, in our family phrase, whitening her tennis shoes: procrastinating, putting off the wonderful, dreadful moment of actually starting to write the damn book.

Quite a lot of it, the notebook shows, was already in my head. Reading *The Day Before Tomorrow* now as if it wasn't written by me – just about possible after all those years – I am rather impressed by its fluency, as if I'd sat down and written it straight off. (Some scenes did come like that, though others had to be worked at, as the notebook makes clear.) What I can see is that, essentially, I didn't know it was difficult to write a novel. I didn't even consider having an unreliable narrator. I didn't feel the need to be postmodern, or modern come to that, or magically realistic, or whatever was in vogue in 1969. This simplicity wasn't approved of by some reviewers, and would doubtless be marked down by academics, but hell, I like it, reading it now.

I think I did get the atmosphere of a hot summer day in Glasgow, though my Glasgow wasn't as simple as (some thought) my characters were. Most reviewers and readers identified the crumbling, derelict Claggans as the Gorbals; interesting, since in my mind it's Cowcaddens. Lisa's library, however, is on the south side, in Govanhill (where I worked for a time). When she leaves work she walks along the broad paths of Victoria Park, which I rather high-handedly moved across the river because, in my mind, its paths were exactly right. But the park where they all meet up on Sunday couldn't be anywhere but Kelvingrove.

The characters were with me from the very beginning. They're listed on page one of the notebook – though Kieron has a different name, and I haven't yet named Lisa, Eugene or Quinn – with a nervous addendum: *I think that's as many as I can manage.* In fact I did at times give other characters a run out – another library assistant, a group of Guide officers (who turned into Helen and Janet), Lisa's boyfriend Clive – but they faded, or never came to life, and I was left with my original group. In this, if in nothing else, I can see a sure instinct at work.

Where did they come from? Mrs Sheehan was a cleaner in one of the libraries I once worked in, who used to tell me about her deadbeat husband – 'Fuckin New Year, Mary,' was his seasonal greeting, which she glossed for me with 'Ma man sweers, ye ken' – with inexhaustible humour, understanding and love. Pat Brady was one, or more, of the old guys in the newspaper room in that library or in any other. He crops up in my writing all the time.

As for the killer, the notebook says some pages in, *what about 'I think they call him Quinn.'* And there he was in my mind, cold and blond. Where on earth did he come from?

Reviewers at the time were in no doubt: he was Bible John, the Glasgow serial killer of the sixties, never found. In an interview on publication day I seem to have staunchly denied this. 'There have been plenty of multi-murderers before the Bible John episode,' the interviewee snippily points out.[1]

Now I'm not quite so sure. I didn't intentionally model Quinn on Bible John. That really would have been simplistic: the fact that the killer was never traced predisposes a writer to much darker thoughts. Where is he now? Is he the nice man next door? I have looked at that possibility in a novella yet to be published, and Ian

Rankin, of course, has done it a million times better in one of his Rebus novels, *Black and Blue*.[2] Yet Bible John was around in Glasgow when I was around, and I don't think I can entirely put aside that influence. Who is he? Where is he? Is he that guy on the bus, the polite one who stands back to let the ladies on? Is he behind you in the queue, in the next cinema seat, in the library reading-room? Somehow, I now think, Bible John did get into my mind, and came out as Quinn.

So the notebook goes on. *Quinn lives alone. And I think we'll have to know pretty early on that he's the killer, e.g. follow him home, his thoughts, thus definitely not detective story.* (This caused a slight hiccup in relations with my otherwise very perceptive editor later on, since she thought it was a detective story and the killer was unmasked too soon. Crossly, I sorted this by unmasking him even sooner.) *Eugene has the mark of doom on him, hasn't he?* And that paragraph runs straight on, like automatic writing, to show how his doom comes about and brings about Quinn's too. That scene was given; it was right as I scribbled it down, and it's still right now. (An academic reader wrote when the book was published: 'I believe that kind of situation where two people keep getting in each other's way is thought to have some sexual significance; had you been thinking of this?' I only wish I had.)

So *The Day Before Tomorrow* was published, on a suitably hot day in July, and on my way home from work I went round all the bookshops in the city centre (four or five, none of them still extant) to see if it was on display. And it was. Moreover, it was reviewed, to an extent you'd hardly believe now; quite favourably, too. 'A degree of confidence and sophistication that augurs well for this writer's future,' said the *Glasgow Herald*. 'Glasgow gothic,' said the *Scotsman* (well, they would). Best of all was Fred Sillitto in the *Scottish Sunday Express*. I never met Fred, and I wish I had, for he got hold of what I was trying to do, which isn't all that common in reviewers. And he liked the way I'd done it. 'It is earthy, poetic and gripping all at once … spiced with humour and graced with a rare economy and delicacy of style.' And Jack House in the *Evening Times* liked the atmospheric Glasgow descriptions; you couldn't ask for more than that.[3]

Readers wrote too. 'I'm glad you had a Janet in the book,' wrote my friend Janet, 'and she remained alive.' One of my mother's coffee-morning acquaintances was reported to like it, but 'she really couldn't judge much as she had never *met* any of that kind of people.' Generally, people read it in one sitting, which was nice; approved of the characters, even those they didn't much like (I never had the energy to pursue this question, though no doubt there was much to know); and thought the Glasgow dialect realistic. Few if any of them were native Glasgow speakers, any more than I was. Post-Tom Leonard, post-Jim Kelman, the dialogue would never pass now.

So what happened next? Well, life, really: a sequence of events which saw me end up as a single mother in the west end of Glasgow, still writing, but not publishing another novel till 1987. That was *Speak, Adam* (the publishers didn't like that title, so it appeared as *A Rumour of Strangers*; it has reverted to its original title for its Kennedy & Boyd reissue this year). It's very different; I like it too. But your first novel is your first novel, and, opening *The Day Before Tomorrow* now, I can still lose myself in the streets of summer Glasgow, green trees and dust and people who might be Mrs Sheehan and might be Quinn.

[1] Jean Smith and Julie Davidson, 'Murder in the Claggans', *Scotsman*, 23 July 1971.

[2] Ian Rankin, *Black and Blue* (Orion, 1997).

[3] Alison Downie, 'Hot week in the city', *Glasgow Herald*, 24 July 1971; Douglas Eadie, 'Glasgow gothic', *Scotsman*, 24 July 1971; Fred Sillitto, 'Moira throws a new light on an old theme', *Scottish Sunday Express*, 25 July 1971; Jack House, 'Bookshelf', *Evening Times*, 3 August 1971.

www.ingramcontent.com/pod-product-compliance
Lightning Source LLC
Chambersburg PA
CBHW030336020726
47493CB00004B/1298